MW01612640

Murder in Blue Gingham

KAREN SUE WALKER

Copyright © 2018 by Karen Sue Walker

All rights reserved.

No part of this book may be reproduced in any form or
by any electronic or mechanical means without written
permission from the author except for the use of brief
quotations in a book review.

This is a work of fiction. All names, characters, locales,
and incidents are products of the author's imagination
and any resemblance to actual people, places, or events
is coincidental.

Visit the author's website at www.karensuewalker.com

To Patti

For reminding me that there are people who love me.

Thank you for being there and always listening.

There are so many people who love you, and I want you to know I'm one of them.

CHAPTER ONE

Max Walters listened to the waves crash against the shore and breathed in the salty sea air as her bare feet sank into the wet sand. Starting her day with a walk on Crystal Shores beach put her in the right frame of mind to face any challenge, big or small.

If she just happened to see Detective Jason Cruz that was an extra bonus. A few weeks ago, when she woke up unusually early (for her), she'd run into him jogging. *He* was jogging. *She* was strolling along the beach looking for sea glass, an activity she'd convinced herself was exercise. Since then, she often started her walk at seven o'clock sharp, hoping she'd see him.

She told herself she liked him as a friend and enjoyed his company, but in her heart she wanted more. Every time she saw him it brightened her day, but she couldn't tell if he had any interest in her. She had once told him she wasn't going to date for a long, long time, but that was last July, nearly a year ago.

She had tried dropping hints, but apparently, she wasn't very good at it. And forget flirting. When other young women were learning how to flirt, she spent years waiting for her childhood friend Andy Fuller to notice her and realize they were meant to be together. It turned out they weren't.

She walked along the shore looking through the pebbles for the telltale glimmer of sea glass when she heard his voice call her name. She turned around.

"Fancy meeting you here," the detective said with a grin.

Max's heart skipped a beat. "It must be such a surprise to see me at this time of the morning, Detective Cruz." He wore a sleeveless tee shirt, which showed off muscles that almost made her melt. He looked every bit the Latin heartthrob with his olive skin and short dark hair, but where had those green eyes come from? They sparkled in the sunlight.

"I wish you would call me Jason," he said, walking alongside of her. "I'm just glad we get to see each other when there's not a murder investigation going on." They had first met when one of her clients was poisoned and collapsed in her shop. Then, last summer, Max had helped him solve another murder that happened at the Crystal Shores Playhouse. Everyone else had thought the actress' death was an accident, but Max's sixth sense told her it wasn't. She managed to convince him to help her find the person responsible.

"I wish you wouldn't say that," Max said. "We've already had two murders in this town. I think that's enough for a lifetime. I know people who have never met a single murderer."

"How dull their lives must be," he said with a laugh. "Actually, I wouldn't mind if my life were a little more dull. I moved to Crystal Shores to get away from crime. I was tired of seeing the bad side of people. I expected to spend the rest of my career investigating petty burglaries and vandalism. What's with this town?"

"Most of us around here are pretty nice," Max said. "And before you arrived, we hadn't had a single murder that I know of. I guess you have bad timing."

"Look there." He stopped and pointed at the pebbles as a wave receded. He dashed over and picked something up. He held his find in the palm of his hand and asked, "Is it sea glass?"

"Yes!" Max said with a grin. She took the piece from his hand and felt a jolt as her skin touched his. She felt her face flush and turned away, hoping he wouldn't notice. "You found a blue piece. Those are so rare." It was a good-sized piece, too. Almost an inch long.

"Beginner's luck," he said.

She held out her palm with the frosty blue glass but he didn't take it from her. Instead, he looked into her eyes with a look she couldn't decipher. "Is something wrong?" she asked, resisting the urge to look away.

"Your eyes," he said.

"My eyes?"

"They're so blue." He looked down at the sea glass in her hand. "Almost the color of that piece of glass in your hand."

He took it from her just as a voice called out his name. He turned toward a woman jogging toward them. With her blond hair in a high ponytail, the woman could be a model for fitness wear. There probably wasn't an ounce of body fat on her.

"There you are," she said to Jason and gave him a kiss on the cheek. "I decided to join you for a run after all. But I see you've found a little friend."

Little friend? Max straightened up to her full height of five foot four inches.

"Max, this is Lori Anderson," Jason said. "Lori, this is Max Walters."

"Oh, you're Max!" Lori exclaimed. "Well, aren't you adorable. Why didn't you tell me how adorable she was, Jason?"

Max managed a half-hearted smile while Jason looked uncomfortable.

"And Jason never told me. Is Max short for Maxine?"

"No, it's just Max," she said with a sigh.

"But really," Lori continued, "what's on your birth certificate?"

"You mean what's my *real* name?" Max had been asked about her name so many times she almost wished her parents had given her a "normal" girl's name. Almost, but not quite. She had learned to like her name. "My birth certificate says Max. Max Elizabeth Walters."

"Well, I think it's very cute."

Adorable? Cute? What was she--a puppy?

"Shall we run?" Jason asked Lori.

"Of course," Lori said. "I suppose I'll see you at the wedding, Max. It's your friend who's getting married, isn't it?"

Max looked at Jason. "You're invited to the wedding?" Her best friend Olivia was getting married in a week, but she hadn't mentioned inviting Jason.

"Yes, Zach invited me."

"You know Zach? How?" Zach was Olivia's fiancé.

"We play poker together on Wednesday nights. Who are you bringing to the wedding?"

"Oh. I'm not bringing a date." Not that she couldn't get a date if she wanted one. At least that's what she told herself. "I'll be too busy with my maid-of-honor duties. Besides, my dad and my friends will be there. I don't need to bring someone. I'll have plenty of people to hang out with." She hoped she didn't sound too defensive.

"Are you not dating anyone?" Lori asked. "Well, that's just wrong. Who do we know who might be right for Max, Jason?" She put her arm in his and snuggled up to him. Max felt awkward witnessing the display of affection. Was Lori trying to let Max know that Jason was off limits? If so, she was doing a good job of it.

Jason seemed to stiffen. "I'm sure Max doesn't need our help finding a date, Lori," he said.

"How about Rob?" she asked Jason. "You remember him, don't you? We ran into him at the bar at Flemings the other night." She turned to Max. "You'd like Rob. He's one of the paralegals at my office."

"Isn't he a little young?" Jason asked.

"So what if he's young?" Lori said, seemingly annoyed that her suggestion wasn't more welcome. "He's a lot of fun. What do you say Max?"

"Um," Max began, not sure what she should say. The last thing she wanted was to be fixed up by Detective Cruz's new girlfriend.

"She's not interested, can't you tell?" Jason said to Lori, then turned to Max. "Do you want to join us on our run?"

"Oh, no. You two go ahead." The only way she'd run would be if someone chased her. Besides, she felt an overwhelming desire to be anywhere else but in their company at that moment. Well. Detective Cruz had a girlfriend. No wonder he hadn't asked her out.

Max watched the two of them run along the shore away from her. Damn. He looked as good from the back as he did from the front. She sighed and walked back toward the street. Today was not starting off to be a good day.

CHAPTER TWO

Crystal Shores was a charming little town of cottages and bungalows where it seemed like everyone knew each other. Coast Highway cut through the middle, but most cars didn't stop on their way from Newport Beach to Laguna Beach. Shop owners wished more of them would visit their boutiques and restaurants, but the local residents enjoyed being overlooked. The beaches were less crowded and you could walk on the street without bumping into crowds of tourists.

An eclectic mix of shops and businesses lined the highway, including Wedding Belles Bridal, Max's shop. Andy Fuller's family bakery stood two doors down between a yarn shop and a realtor that featured million dollar homes. Sadly, Crystal Shores bungalows were slowly being torn down and replaced by mini mansions, changing the feel of the town. Progress was inevitable, but that didn't mean that Max had to be happy about it.

She unlocked the front door of Wedding Belles at nine thirty. Now that she owned the shop, she arrived early to prepare for her day. Stepping into the bridal salon, she couldn't help smiling at the transformation she had made with the help of her friend Eric Mancini.

Eric owned the flower shop a few doors down, and he had helped her redecorate after she bought the shop from her previous boss almost a year ago. Max insisted that the focal point be an exquisite rug her father had given her. Years ago, her late mother had fallen in love with it and brought it back from Nepal, even though it was too big for their living room. It was just the right size for the shop and it made Max smile to have something of her mother's here where she could see it every day. The rug had a floral pattern with shades of pink and pale green, and it was the perfect inspiration for the redecoration.

The white walls had been repainted in a pale shade of blush, and she had replaced the wall-to-wall carpeting with whitewashed oak floors. Eric tried to talk her into contemporary furniture, but Max held out for a softer look, and they settled on a pale green velvet love seat and matching armchairs in a classic style. A long row of wedding dresses lined one side of the showroom, and glass displays of tiaras and headpieces stood against the other wall. Photos of some of her custom-designed wedding gowns were artfully framed and hung around the room.

She loved the way her showroom looked, but every morning when she stepped in the door, she stood there for several moments trying to figure out what was missing. Oh well, it would come to her one day. She often tried hard to figure out the answer to a problem and then it just popped into her head when she wasn't even thinking about it.

Max checked the schedule on the computer. There were three appointments for the day: two brides looking for gowns and one first fitting for a bride who planned a July wedding. She'd ordered from one of the many designers Max carried, as most of her clients did. Only a few brides special ordered custom gowns, but Max was well known for her design abilities. She'd attended a prestigious design school in L.A., and worked for a famous designer in New York before her mother became ill, but most of her skills had been learned right here at Wedding Belles where she had worked since she was a teenager. She felt proud of what she had accomplished at the age of twenty-nine. She never thought she'd own her own business at such a young age, and she never could have done it without the support of her friends, family, and former boss.

Besides her reputation as a wedding gown designer, Max was also known for being able to find the perfect gown for almost any bride. This special skill had earned her extra attention, and now most of her business came from word of mouth. The Internet was full of glowing reviews for her and her shop.

Max didn't need her schedule to tell her that her dear friend Olivia Cavendish was coming in later for her final fitting. She couldn't wait to see Olivia in the gown she'd designed.

A few minutes before ten, the back door opened.

"I'm here," Keiko Hamasaki, her assistant, called out. She came into the office to put her bag away. "Oh," she said, looking over Max's shoulder. "Is Olivia coming in today?"

"Yes," Max grinned, taking a quick look at Keiko's outfit.

Keiko was Max's opposite in so many ways, but they got along so well it was like they were meant to work together. Keiko, who was half Japanese, liked to dress very uniquely in various styles inspired by Japanese fashion trends. It drove the previous owner batty, but Max looked forward to seeing what she would be wearing each day. Today, she wore a powder blue baby doll dress and four-inch platform shoes. Her hair was in two French braids with big blue bows on the ends.

"Is it going to be a busy day or a super busy day?" Keiko asked. Saturdays were never quiet.

"I think just a busy day, unless we get lots of drop-ins."

"I will handle the drop-ins today," Keiko informed her in a very serious manner. "You are too nice. People need to know that they can't just stop by a bridal shop on a Saturday and expect to be accommodated."

Keiko had a point. Max was a bit of a pushover, but she hated turning business away. The shop had done well since the grand re-opening ten months ago, but she couldn't help worrying now that it was her responsibility to pay the bills.

"Okay, but be nice about it when you tell them we can't help them today."

"When am I not nice?" Keiko asked, but the truth was she had a tendency to be blunt, unlike Max. People often told Max she was too nice, but they rarely accused Keiko of that. Not everyone liked it when you spoke to them in a direct, no nonsense manner the way Keiko did. Max found it refreshing. "I will be so nice, they will thank me for not helping them today. I will convince them it will be so much better if they make an appointment for another day."

"Okay, I'm willing to try it out. The drop-ins are all yours today. Olivia is coming in at four for her final fitting. Things should have calmed down by then."

Keiko grinned. "I am excited to see her in her wedding gown. Is she bringing anyone with her today?"

"No one else gets to see it until Saturday, not even her mother. I can't wait until everyone watches her walk down the aisle." Max went to the front door and turned the sign around to OPEN.

By the time her friend Olivia was due to arrive, Max had to admit that Keiko's way was better. Usually she was exhausted on Saturdays from trying to help everyone who walked in the door. And Keiko had made three appointments for the following week.

Keiko and Max were hanging up dresses when a young woman burst through the door. "You've got to help me," she pleaded.

Max was alarmed. "What's wrong?"

"Antoine's Bridal has shut their doors," the woman said, nervously twisting the handle of her purse as she spoke. "They've gone bankrupt and I can't get my dress. I've already paid for it and I can't reach anyone to find out if I can get a refund. I've called and emailed but they're not responding at all. I'm getting married in three weeks and I don't have a dress!"

"I don't know how I can help," Max said, shocked to hear the news about her competitor. Antoine's Bridal was one of the biggest bridal boutique chains on the West Coast. They had opened several new stores just in the last year. "Why did they go out of business?"

"I don't know," the woman said. "I just know they've declared bankruptcy and it will be months before any of us get our money back, if we ever do."

Keiko stepped up to them. "We can make an appointment for you." She held her laptop in one hand. "How's Wednesday?"

"Um, does that mean you can help?" the woman asked hopefully.

"Max is a miracle worker. I'm sure she can help," Keiko said confidently.

"Oh, thank you!" A smile took over her face. "I'll come whenever you can fit me in."

"Wednesday at eleven," Keiko said. "What's your name?"

"I'm Charlotte." She reached out her hand.

Keiko put her laptop on the coffee table and shook hands with Charlotte. "I'm Keiko, and this is Max." Keiko sat down and started typing on her computer.

"I'm not sure," Max said, not feeling as confident as Keiko. She didn't want to make an appointment for the woman only to tell her she couldn't do anything for her.

Charlotte turned to Max, the smile fading. "You're my last hope. You've got to help me. I've been everywhere else and no one seems to care that my wedding is going to be ruined." She sounded desperate.

"It's just that three weeks isn't much time," Max said. It was barely time to do alterations, much less order a dress.

Tears filled Charlotte's eyes. "What am I going to do?" she wailed as her eyes filled with tears. "I'm going to have to cancel the wedding. I'm going to lose all my deposits. And what about the honeymoon? We can't go on our honeymoon if we're not married." She plopped down on the sofa and put her head in her hands sobbing.

Keiko appeared with a box of tissues and glared at Max as if this was all her fault. What did she expect? No matter what Keiko said, she couldn't work miracles.

Max watched Charlotte dab at her eyes, her makeup smeared. It broke her heart to see her in such distress.

"Let me see if I can think of something, Charlotte," Max said. "Give me a few days."

Charlotte jumped up from the sofa and threw her arms around Max and said, "Bless you!"

"I can't promise anything," Max said, not wanting to get her hopes up. "Antoine's was the only place I know of that had a selection of off-the-rack dresses you could buy." Most bridal shops, like Wedding Belles, had gowns for brides to try on then ordered them from the designer. They only sold the out of date dresses at sample sales usually held twice a year.

Max didn't know how she could help on such short notice, but she wrote down Charlotte's phone number and email address and told her she'd let her know what ideas she came up with.

After Charlotte left, Keiko said, "You were supposed to let me make appointments. You are not being very helpful."

"You're not serious, are you?" One look at Keiko told Max that she was. "Sorry. I just don't know if we can help her and I didn't want to get her hopes up."

"You will think of something. You always do."

While Max appreciated that Keiko believed in her so strongly, she had her doubts. But Max believed in fairy tale weddings and as far as she was concerned the perfect wedding gown was at the center of any wedding. A bride depended on her. She had to think of something, and fast!

oOo

Few things made Max Walters happier than a glowing bride to be in a gown she'd created, and when it was her best friend, that just made it even better. Sweet, gentle Olivia had taken over as artistic director at the Crystal Shores Playhouse a year ago. She met her fiancé Zach at the Playhouse when he performed in a small part in *Romeo and Juliet* last summer when she was still the stage manager. Zach said it was love at first sight. It took Olivia a little longer, but then she was never one to rush into anything. It wasn't long before she admitted to Max that she was head over heels in love with him, too.

Max had designed her most beautiful dress yet for her friend. She was Olivia's maid of honor, so she'd been very busy getting ready for the wedding next weekend. Max wanted the gown to be her wedding gift to her friend, but Olivia had insisted on paying for the cost of the materials. She said that way she wouldn't feel guilty about choosing the most expensive fabrics and trims.

Max knew that once everyone in town saw Olivia's gown, her custom orders would only increase. Besides wedding gowns, some well-to-do locals had started asking her to create gowns for formal functions. Max was having trouble keeping up with the workload already, but she would never complain about having too many orders.

Olivia's off-the-shoulder dress was cut on the bias, which made it fit the slender bride-to-be beautifully. Max had found just the right shade of ivory with a touch of pink to complement Olivia's pale complexion. Her dark, silky hair fell sleekly to her waist.

Keiko oohed and aahed as Olivia beamed while viewing herself in six tall mirrors in what Max liked to call the Dream Room. Olivia stood on the pedestal in the center of the room.

She spun around and the skirt flared out then settled back into silky folds.

"You've outdone yourself, Max," Olivia said. "I feel like a goddess. You totally got the Forties feel that I asked for. I just didn't expect it to be so glamorous. Thank you. Both of you."

"Max deserves all the credit," Keiko said. "I only sewed a few seams. But on second thought, I will accept your gratitude. That satin was exceptionally difficult to work with."

"Keiko is being diplomatic." Max said, checking over the gown to make sure the fit was flawless. She wanted this gown to be perfect. "Silk satin is a challenge, slipping all over the place while you try to sew it. But the end result is worth the extra effort." In fact, it was a real pain in the you-know-what to work with, but Max wouldn't tell Olivia that. She rarely sewed with it because most brides chose less expensive options. But it was what Olivia wanted, and Max couldn't be happier with the final result.

"How are you going to wear your hair?" Keiko asked. "You're not wearing a veil or tiara or anything are you?"

"No, I'm not a tiara kind of girl," Olivia said. Her style was much more understated and classic. "I thought I'd just wear my hair down. Zach likes it that way." Her face lit up at the mere mention of his name.

"Well, if Zach likes it that way…" Max teased. She fully approved of Olivia's choice in husband, partly because he was a great guy, but mostly because Olivia loved him with all her heart. She hoped to feel that way someday.

"I happen to like to make him happy," Olivia said with a grin. "Besides, not having some fancy hairstyle is one less thing to worry about."

"Are you sure?" Max had her doubts. "It will probably be breezy at the beach. It could be downright windy, for all you know."

"I hadn't thought of that," Olivia said.

"That's why you have me as your maid of honor. To think of all the things you don't. Do you really want to say your vows while trying to keep your hair out of your face?"

Keiko piped in. "She's got a point."

"So tell me, what do you two suggest?" Olivia asked.

"A simple updo would be nice," Max said. "Perhaps a French twist."

Keiko looked thoughtful. "Yes, that would work nicely. You can always take it down after the ceremony."

"I guess I'll need to call the hair salon then. I'm not going to try to do it myself. Shall I make an appointment for the two of you, too? We could go together."

"Not me," Keiko said, recoiling slightly. "I don't let anyone touch my hair."

Max glanced at Keiko with amusement. She almost always had her hair in braids, pigtails, or two buns perched on top of her head like mouse ears. "I'm in," Max told Olivia. "We didn't make any appointments for the shop on Saturday. We don't even have to open if we don't want to. That's one of the benefits of having a small shop in a small town."

"And being your own boss," Olivia added.

The front door jingled, and Max left the two women and entered the showroom to see who had arrived. A petite young woman around her age stood in torn jeans and a loose flannel shirt. Her shoulder-length mousy brown hair was tucked behind her ears. Max was intrigued by the suitcase she pulled behind her, since brides didn't usually bring luggage to shop for a wedding gown.

"May I help you?" Max asked.

Keiko rushed into the showroom. "Would you like to make an appointment?"

"I'm looking for Olivia," she said in a thick East Coast accent. "I went by the theater where she works and they told me she was here."

Olivia came into the room and squealed, "Gabby! I thought I heard your voice. What are you doing here?"

"What kind of a greeting is that?" Gabby said, and stepped forward to hug Olivia. "Look what a beautiful bride you are! I couldn't miss out on your special day, now could I?"

"This is wonderful! I'm so glad you changed your mind. But you said you weren't coming. You said you couldn't get off work."

"Yeah, well, we'll see if I still have a job when I get back home."

"Gabby!" Olivia sounded concerned.

"It's okay. I wanted to surprise you. And by the look on your face, I've succeeded. I know how much you love being surprised." Gabby snickered at her joke.

Max knew Olivia hated surprises and figured Gabby knew also, but Olivia seemed to be taking it well.

"Keiko, Max, this is Gabrielle Karsten," Olivia said. "Max is my maid of honor."

"Great to meet you. Olivia's told me all about you two. Call me Gabby," she said, reaching out to shake both their hands with a firm grip. "Everyone does. I tried for years to break them of the habit, but I finally gave up."

Max noticed a beautiful ring with a green stone on Gabby's hand as they shook. "What a gorgeous ring," she said. "What kind of stone is it?"

"It's an emerald. My grandmother left it to me when she passed away."

"Oh, I'm sorry," Max said.

"It was years ago," Gabby said. "But I like having the ring to remind me of her."

"So you and Olivia have known each other a long time," Max said, changing the subject.

"Sure have. We grew up together in Hoboken and went to the same college."

"You went to Berkeley, too?" Max asked, wondering why Olivia had never mentioned her childhood friend had gone to the same college she had.

"Yep. Somehow, I managed to get a scholarship. The two of us moved across the country together. We even shared a dorm room for a bit." Max detected a note of wistfulness in her voice, as if she missed the old times. "When do Quinn and Ashley get into town?" she asked.

"Later today. They're driving down from San Francisco. Did you know Quinn got married?" When Gabby shook her head, Olivia continued. "She married Nicholas Buckley."

"Nicky? Quinn married Nicky?" Gabby said gleefully. "What a kick!"

"You knew him?" Olivia said, raising her eyebrows.

"Yeah, we hooked up in college. It wasn't anything major, but I bet Quinn wouldn't want to hear about it. You know how jealous she gets. I didn't even know Quinn knew Nicky."

"She met him after college," Olivia said. "She'll be surprised to hear you knew him before she did."

"I bet she will," Gabby said mischievously.

Max didn't think it would take too much prompting to get Gabby to tell them all her secrets. She was definitely a talker and didn't seem to have much of a filter, but Olivia didn't try to get her to spill, disappointing Max a little. People fascinated Max, and she always wanted to know their stories and their secrets.

"I hope you're not going to make any trouble," Olivia said, frowning.

Max wondered where that comment came from. Did Gabby have a habit of making trouble?

"Me? Make trouble?" Gabby laughed, a little too loudly. "Of course not. So where is the gang staying?" Gabby didn't wait for an answer. "Some swanky hotel, I suppose. Nicky made so much freaking money on those books of his, he can afford it. I keep waiting for him to write another one, but I suppose he lost interest after his entire family died."

Max looked at Olivia with surprise. She'd never told Max anything about Nicholas's background besides the fact that he'd written the bestselling *Immersion* trilogy that had been a huge phenomenon a few years earlier. How tragic for him to lose his family.

"They rented a house on the beach," Olivia said. "We're invited over this evening. I'll let them know you're coming." She turned to head back to the dressing room to get her phone.

"Oh, please don't," Gabby pleaded. "I want to see Nicky's face when he recognizes me."

"Where are you staying?" Max asked Gabby. "Can we give you a ride to your hotel?"

"Don't be silly. I'm staying with Olivia."

Max would have laughed at the look on Olivia's face if she thought her friend wouldn't kill her later. With all the last minute wedding preparations, the last thing Olivia needed was an unexpected houseguest. But Olivia smiled bravely and said, "Of course. I wouldn't have it any other way."

Something bothered Max. She turned to Olivia. "If you grew up together, why does Gabby have an accent and you don't?"

Gabby didn't give Olivia a chance to answer. "Olivia hated that New Jersey accent. We both took speech classes to get rid of it, but I never could. Don't get me wrong. I tried. After all, who's going to give a role in a Shakespeare play to someone who sounds like me?" She laughed. "That would be a hoot!"

"Let me change back into my street clothes," Olivia mumbled to no one in particular and went back to the dressing room. Max followed her, leaving Keiko to make small talk with Gabby. She knew Keiko would have some more details about the new arrival to share with her when they were alone.

"So you didn't know she was coming?" Max asked Olivia.

"No, she said she couldn't come. I really am glad to see her," she said sincerely, but Max could tell she had reservations. "It's just that everything is planned to a T, and now I'm going to have to change the rehearsal dinner reservations and I don't know what else. I hope she doesn't expect to be a bridesmaid. I had asked her when I first got engaged, but she said she couldn't come so I pared the list down to three—you, Quinn, and Ashley."

"I'm sure she doesn't expect to be a bridesmaid showing up at the last minute like this," Max said.

"Oh, you don't know Gabby." Olivia shook her head slowly. "She'd try to guilt me into it and then ask to borrow a dress." She frowned. "I'm making her sound like a terrible person. She's really not. She's just a free spirit and she doesn't always think things through. She was my best friend growing up. She talked me into so many adventures I can't even remember them all. And we only got caught a few times." She smiled at the memory.

"She got you into trouble?" Max couldn't believe her ears. Olivia followed every rule and never ruffled any feathers.

"Yes, can you believe it? She really got me out of my shell. I was so shy when I was a kid."

After Olivia and Gabby left, Keiko filled her in. "So, Gabby was also a theater major like Olivia, but she didn't keep her grades up so she lost her scholarship and had to leave college. It sounds like she didn't show up to class most of the time. I sensed that she had some problems with alcohol or drugs. She didn't admit it, but she hinted at it. She seems very bright, but I sense that she's a bit jealous of Olivia."

"Why would you come all the way from New Jersey to be at the wedding of a friend you're jealous of?" Max wondered aloud.

"Oh, I think she really cares about her. She just wishes she had Olivia's life. It sounds like she had it rough growing up and

21

used to go to Olivia's house just to get a decent meal and some peace."

"You got all that out of her just while Olivia was changing?"

"I guess my interrogation skills are improving," Keiko said impishly. "I learned from the best."

"Well, I think you've got me beat. Are you coming with me tonight?" Max said.

"I wouldn't miss it for anything," Keiko said. "I want to meet the rest of Olivia's friends. If Gabby is any indication, this should be an interesting evening."

They finished straightening up the shop, and before they knew it, it was six o'clock and time to close.

"Are you ready to go, or do you need to go home first?" Max asked Keiko.

"Let me touch up my mascara and I'll be ready," Keiko said.

Max thought Keiko had plenty of mascara on, and started to say so, but remembered her own mother criticizing her for wearing too much makeup, and decided not to say anything. The memory made Max tear up. Nearly two years after losing her mother to cancer, she still got weepy at random times, whenever a memory would sneak up on her. She wished she could hear her mother's voice one more time, even if it were telling her that her skirt was too short or she needed to eat better.

After adding another layer of mascara to her eyelashes, Keiko asked Max, "Are you wearing that?"

Max laughed. It was just the sort of thing her mother would have said. "What's wrong with what I'm wearing?" She had chosen the cream-colored sleeveless blouse, red slacks and tan sweater with the idea she could wear them after work.

Keiko scrunched up her face. "Take off the sweater," she suggested.

Max took off her sweater and Keiko nodded her approval. She reached into her messenger bag and pulled out a necklace with a pendant.

"Did you make this?" Max turned the pendant over in her hand, admiring the gold filigree holding a red stone. "It's the Chintamani, isn't it?"

Keiko grinned. "Since no one claimed it, I decided to make you a necklace. There may yet be some good luck in it, even if you used up your three wishes."

Keiko believed the gemstone Max had found on the beach last summer was a magic wishing stone. Max didn't usually believe in such things, but this stone had a special meaning for her.

Keiko helped her put the necklace on and it sparkled on her chest.

"It's beautiful," Max said. "Thank you. Hopefully, I won't need any luck tonight."

"I am looking forward to meeting the rest of Olivia's friends. Something tells me it will not be a boring evening. Gabby seems like someone who will ruffle a few feathers."

"That's true," Max said, brightening. "It could be very interesting."

"Are we bringing the bridesmaids dresses?" Keiko asked.

"Thank you for reminding me." Max went to the workroom and pulled Quinn and Ashley's dresses off the rack. They had emailed her their measurements and she had finished sewing them just a few days ago. She hadn't gotten around to completing her own. In fact she'd barely started it, but she wasn't concerned since she had an entire week before it had to be done. She'd sewn a dress in a single day, after all, not that she really wanted to try that again. They didn't have any appointments on Wednesday, so she could get most of it done then. Yes, she had plenty of time.

CHAPTER THREE

Max and Keiko stopped at the wine shop for a bottle of wine to bring to the get-together. Max cringed at paying twenty dollars for a bottle of Chardonnay, since it cost more than she usually paid, but she didn't want Olivia's friends to think she was cheap.

Keiko pulled up in front of the house, a huge salmon-colored Mediterranean-style villa with a tiny front yard. They walked up the stone walkway and rang the doorbell. The mahogany door slowly opened and they were greeted by a woman with long, wavy, strawberry blond hair.

"You must be Max and Keiko," the woman said. "I'm Ashley."

Ashley was dressed casually in yoga pants and tank top. She led them past an enormous kitchen. Max stopped in her tracks. Her entire apartment would fit in the living area. At the opposite side of the room, floor to ceiling windows afforded a one-hundred-eighty-degree view of the coastline from Long Beach to Laguna.

"Wow," Keiko said. Wow was right.

"Olivia's late. So unlike her. Quinn and Nicholas are on the veranda." Ashley took the bridesmaids' dresses from Max, and pulled one of them out of the plastic that covered it. It was a simple floor length gown with spaghetti straps in a pale shade of silvery blue.

"I love it," she said. "What a pretty color."

"It's really going to complement your coloring," Max said. She had seen pictures of the two sisters before she picked the shade of blue for their dresses. "Quinn's, too."

"What color is your dress?" Ashley asked. "Is it different since you're the maid of honor?"

"It's blue, too. Just a darker shade."

Ashley grinned. "You know how the bride always tells her bridesmaids they'll be able to wear the dress again?"

Max laughed. "And they never can. I still have a hideous bridesmaid's dress in the back of my closet that I've been meaning to get rid of for years. It's yellow, and I look awful in yellow, like I have jaundice or something. I think that's part of why I'm so careful about picking the right colors for bridesmaids."

"I think I will actually wear this one again. It will be nice to have something to wear if I need something formal."

"I'm shortening mine to just above the knee after the wedding," Max said. She didn't expect to get invited to any formal events anytime soon.

Ashley took the two dresses to one of the back rooms and returned moments later volunteering to put the wine in the refrigerator. "Nicholas made a very large pitcher of martinis. Good thing none of us have to work tomorrow."

Max was curious to meet Nicholas, the famous novelist, especially after learning about his family tragedy. She and Keiko followed Ashley outside to the veranda.

"This is my sister Quinn." Max reached out to shake her hand as Quinn stood up. Her dark pixie cut hair and high cheekbones gave her a mischievous look. She looked stylish in a crisp white shirt and navy shorts. A man, obviously Nicholas, leaned against the railing staring out at the sea. Max eyed him curiously. His head was completely shaved and he seemed to be ignoring everyone. Was he rude or perhaps just shy?

"So, you're the one who replaced me as Olivia's best friend," Quinn said, smiling.

"Well, um…" Max didn't know quite what to say.

"Don't listen to her," Ashley said. "She's precocious. That's a nice way to say it, isn't it Quinn?" Quinn just laughed in response.

"What a lovely necklace," Quinn said. "Is it a ruby?"

Max grinned. "No, nothing that valuable. Although this stone has a special value to me. I found it on the beach one day while I was looking for sea glass."

"Don't even ask her about sea glass," Keiko said, "or you will learn way more than you ever wanted to know."

"Hey," Max said. "I happen to think it's very interesting."

Keiko just shook her head. Max decided to keep her information about sea glass to herself. For now.

"Nicholas," Quinn called out, "come meet Max and Keiko." Nicholas stopped staring out at the ocean and came over to them. He had sleepy, gray eyes that made him look slightly bored. Or maybe he was bored. Max guessed he was in his early thirties from what she'd been told, but he looked older somehow. He wore loose fitting jeans, a tee shirt, and flip flops.

He greeted them, shook both their hands, and then poured them vodka martinis. "I'm sorry I don't have any olives. Quinn is usually so good at taking care of things, but apparently, she forgot them. I think a martini without olives is like…" He paused, searching for the right phrase.

"Like a Mai Tai without the umbrella?" Quinn said, finishing his sentence.

"Exactly. How is it that you always know exactly what I'm going to say? I'd be hopeless without you." He leaned over and kissed his wife on the cheek. "Although it's quite uncharacteristic of you to forget olives."

The doorbell rang and Ashley went to get it. Quinn said, "That's either Olivia or dinner. We couldn't decide who should cook, so we gave up and ordered in. Besides, who wants to clean pots and pans on a vacation?"

"You have pots and pans?" Keiko asked.

"Yes," Nicholas said. "This place came completely furnished, and it's cheaper than staying at the Ritz. Plus it's closer to Olivia. Do you know you don't have any hotels in Crystal Shores?"

Of course Max knew there weren't any hotels in her town. And even if there were, she suspected they wouldn't meet Nicholas's standards. He must have made a ton of money on the books he'd written to be able to afford to stay at the Ritz.

"I hope our little town doesn't disappoint you." Max hoped she didn't sound defensive. She loved Crystal Shores.

"Your town is charming," Quinn said. "I think this is so much nicer than a hotel. The beach is right here and we've got room to entertain. I'm much happier here than I would have been at the Ritz."

"Our beach is much nicer than the one at the Ritz," Keiko said. "And less crowded, especially at this end of the beach. Hardly anyone comes down this far."

Ashley reappeared on the veranda with Olivia and Gabby at her side. Max expected the surprised looks on everyone's faces, but didn't know what to think about the lack of surprise on the part of Nicholas. Did he not recognize her or was he pretending not to know Gabby for Quinn's sake? Max didn't think it would do him much good, since she didn't expect Gabby to keep quiet.

Olivia wore tan linen shorts and a lacy white tee over a camisole. Max recognized the checkered sundress Gabby wore, since it was one of Olivia's. It was just like Olivia to loan her friend something to wear. Olivia was generous to a fault, and she seemed to have a soft spot for Gabby.

"It's me!" Gabby said gleefully the moment she stepped onto the veranda. "Am I the last person you expected to see?" Gabby obviously enjoyed surprising everyone.

Quinn recovered quickly and gave her old college friend a hug. "You're not the last person I expected to see, Gabby, but I am surprised. Olivia said you couldn't come." She turned to Olivia. "Did you know she was in town?"

"Don't be mad at her," Gabby said, grinning. "I showed up today without telling anyone, and I made her promise not to tell. You look fabulous, Quinn. Love the short hair." She walked up to Nicholas. "Hi, Nicky! Wow, you've changed. You always had long hair and a beard. I remember you said you hated razors. Don't you remember me? How 'bout a hug for old times' sake?"

"Hi, Gabby," Nicholas said, and gave her a reluctant embrace. Gabby held on a bit longer than might be considered appropriate. After Gabby released him, he said, "I go by Nicholas now."

"Oh, but you'll always be Nicky to me." Gabby stared at him curiously, as if having trouble getting used to how much he'd changed in eight years.

"You two know each other?" Quinn asked with surprise.

"We met in college," Gabby said. "I hung out with his roommate for a while."

This was a different story from what she had told Olivia earlier that day. Perhaps she was considering Quinn's feelings.

"You knew him in college?" Quinn asked. "That's before I even met him."

"Yeah, well, he doesn't even remember me, so I must not have made much of an impression," Gabby said. "Now, what does a girl have to do around here to get a drink?"

"Where's Zach?" Quinn asked. "I thought we were going to meet him tonight."

"He's on a business trip for a few days," Olivia said. "You'll meet him later in the week."

"Well, that's disappointing," Ashley said. "We were looking forward to quizzing him and making sure he was good enough for you."

"She doesn't mean that," Quinn said.

"Yes, I do," Ashley huffed. "Don't tell me what I mean."

"Okay, you two," Olivia interrupted their spat. "Sometimes you make me glad I don't have a sister."

Ashley laughed. "We only argue because we love each other." She hugged her sister, and there seemed to be no hard feelings.

Was that what it was like to have a sibling? Max, like Olivia, was an only child. She looked over at Keiko, who raised her eyebrows as if to say she'd warned Max things would get interesting.

"Now what about that drink?" Gabby asked. Apparently, patience wasn't one of her virtues.

Nicholas poured her a drink and the six women crowded around the glass table under the shade of the umbrella while he stretched out in the Adirondack chair soaking up the sun, his eyes obscured by sunglasses.

"This is like old times," Olivia said, smiling. "All we need is a deck of cards."

Gabby laughed. "I could take all your spare change like I used to. You were terrible card players. Except for Quinn. She has a world-class poker face. You can never tell what she's really thinking."

Quinn looked at her unsmiling. "Are you saying I'm a liar?"

Olivia leaned forward as if to step in if things went too far.

"That's not what I'm saying," Gabby said with a grin. "Come on, Quinn. Lighten up. This is a reunion for us. No need for bad blood between us." Gabby waited for a response, but got none. "Let's make up and be friends. It's about time, don't you think?"

Max wondered what Gabby meant by that and waited to see Quinn's reaction.

A slow smile crept over Quinn's face. "Oh, I can't stay mad at you, Gabby. I never could."

Olivia leaned back in her chair, seemingly relieved that the tension had lifted. Had she stopped the two from fighting in the past? And what did Gabby mean by "bad blood"?

Max glanced over at Keiko who merely shrugged.

CHAPTER FOUR

Max liked to have a drink now and then, but these people could really drink. Olivia slowly nursed her second martini and Max and Keiko had switched to sparkling water, but the others showed no signs of slowing down, especially Gabby. Quinn and Ashley asked Olivia questions about Zach—how they met and fell in love. Olivia's face lit up when she talked about him.

Max watched and listened, taking it all in. Gabby kept stealing glances at Nicholas, and Max became more curious to know what their relationship had been. She wondered what Quinn would think if she learned what had really gone on between Gabby and her husband. It was long before they were married, but if Quinn were the jealous type, it might still bug her.

Quinn sat stiffly in her chair, her hands folded in her lap except when she reached for her drink. Was she always this uptight? Ashley seemed so different from her sister, one minute slouching back in her chair and the next leaning forward and waving her hands around as she talked.

Gabby told a story about Olivia and her climbing down into the storm drains looking for crocodiles that the neighborhood kids had said lurked down there.

"I remember that," Olivia said. "I always wondered who started that rumor. All the kids believed it."

Gabby started to snicker.

"You?" Olivia asked in a mock accusatory voice. "All this time and you never told me it was you?"

Gabby laughed out loud and Ashley and Quinn laughed with her. Olivia joined in as if she couldn't help herself. Max didn't know if it was the story or the liquor, but soon the four college friends were out of breath from laughing. Keiko sipped her mineral water and looked as if she didn't know what was so funny. Max thought it was nice to see them reconnecting, all the tension between them seemingly having evaporated into thin air.

Max slipped back inside the house. She needed to use the ladies room, and decided to take advantage of the opportunity to look around. She hoped no one would mind if she was caught checking out the place. Besides, it wasn't their home, so it wasn't really snooping, was it? She wondered how much a house like this cost to rent. A fortune, she guessed. Maybe she'd ask Olivia later.

There were four large bedrooms, the largest of which had a bathroom to die for with a whirlpool tub and glass enclosed shower with multiple showerheads. Max nearly drooled. Her own bathroom was the size of a small closet, and not the walk-in type. She couldn't help but feel the towels, which were as fluffy as they looked. Max opened the medicine cabinet, even though she told herself she shouldn't, but only found a stick of deodorant, two toothbrushes, and a tube of toothpaste. There was an electric shaver on the counter, and Max wondered if Nicholas used it to shave his head. Perhaps he was going bald.

Max returned to the veranda just as the Italian food Nicholas had ordered arrived. Gabby finished her martini and asked Nicholas to pour her another. She tried to coax Max and Keiko into accepting another drink as if it were her mission to see that

33

they all got plastered. She prattled on while they ate, talking about their college days and the plays they used to do together. Max enjoyed hearing about Olivia's life before she met her.

Gabby gulped down her second martini. "It's not often you get to see your old pals when you haven't heard from them in eight years," she said in a voice that was beginning to slur. "Eight long years, and not a word, except for dear, sweet, loyal Olivia." Gabby glared at Nicholas while she said this. "I feel as if I don't even know you at all." Was the comment meant for all of her schoolmates or just Nicholas?

Quinn protested that she had meant to call but then lost her number. "I tried to connect with you online, but you didn't respond. That's how I keep in touch with pretty much everyone these days."

Gabby laughed loudly and said, "I'm only giving you trouble. You know me. I was always trouble."

"That's not true," Olivia said. "You've just had some tough times, that's all. The important thing is we're all here together now."

Nicholas left the room to mix another pitcher of martinis, and Gabby followed him into the kitchen.

"You've got to check out the rest of the house," Max whispered to Keiko. "It's gorgeous."

Keiko excused herself and returned shortly afterward. She had a pained look on her face that Max hadn't seen before. "I'm so sorry," she said, "but I seem to have a migraine. I'm afraid I need to leave the party early. It was so nice to meet all of you."

Max had never known Keiko to have so much as a headache, much less a migraine. She was about to say so when she realized

34

that Keiko must be looking for an excuse to leave early. "Are you going to be okay driving? I know how you get with these migraines."

Max saw the hint of a smile on Keiko's face, before it was replaced again by the pained look of suffering.

"I can drive myself home. Can you get a ride?"

"Olivia can drive me home, right Olivia?" When her friend nodded, Max said, "I'll walk you to the car."

Once they were standing on the street by the car, Max asked, "Okay, what's up?"

"I'm meeting someone," Keiko said evasively, "but I wanted to tell you what I overheard before I forgot it."

"What did you hear?"

"It was Gabby and Nicholas. Or should I say Nicky? Did you notice how much he hated being called that?"

"I sure did," Max agreed. "So what did they say?"

"Gabby said 'I think Quinn would be interested in the truth.'"

"Truth about what?"

"I don't know," Keiko admitted, "but he said 'what do you want from me?'"

"Really. Well, that's interesting."

"I thought so. I didn't hear the rest. Enjoy the fireworks."

Max went back into the house. She arrived just in time to see Gabby stumble down to the beach in a huff, a large cup in one hand and a beach towel in the other.

"What's with her?" Max wondered out loud.

"I blame it on the vodka," Ashley said from the kitchen where she poured herself a glass of wine. "And she took another

35

drink with her. Let's not let her spoil our fun. This is my first vacation in a year and I plan to enjoy it. What time does the sun set?"

"Not until close to eight thirty this time of the year," Olivia said, coming in through the sliding glass doors. "We've got over an hour of sunlight left to be followed by one of our glorious sunsets. I've ordered up an especially spectacular one for you tonight."

Max decided not to ask when the fireworks were expected.

oOo

Max thought it was more than too much vodka that had set Gabby off, and she planned to find out what had happened as she, Ashley, and Olivia joined everyone else back on the veranda. "So, what did I miss? Gabby looked angry."

"It's me, I'm afraid," Nicholas admitted, the sun reflecting on his sunglasses. "I wanted to talk to Quinn alone, but we're all friends, right?" He didn't sound convincing. "Gabby and I went out in college." He turned to Quinn and took her hand. "I'm sorry, but before I met you, I wasn't that picky about who I went out with. It was over almost as soon as it began. No one broke it off. We just started seeing other people."

"So why was she angry then?" Quinn asked her husband.

"She was annoyed that I was being indifferent toward her. I don't know what she expected. I told her I didn't want any trouble." He looked at Quinn with a pleading look in his eyes. "I didn't want to tell you, but I figured you'd rather hear it from me than from her. Forgive me?"

She shook her head as if she were ready to scold him, and then said, "Of course. I have a past, too, you know."

Ashley erupted in laughter, startling Max. "Sure you do, Miss Goody Two-Shoes."

"Hey! I dated other people before I met my Nicholas."

Nicholas took Quinn in his arms and held her closely. "Things could get uncomfortable. I wonder if I should go and apologize."

"I don't think that's necessary," Ashley said.

Quinn disagreed. "I think you should. Let her know it's out in the open. She comes off so tough, but I know she's not really. Not with everything she's been through. Tell her I'm not upset. I don't want her to think I'm angry."

"She's drunk," Ashley said. "Let her sober up and then talk to her."

Max thought Ashley had a point. She didn't understand why Nicholas was so eager to talk with Gabby.

"She wasn't that drunk," Nicholas said, standing up. "I'll be back shortly." He walked down the steps to the beach and headed south.

Max looked out at the shoreline, but didn't see Gabby anywhere. She must have found a spot on the other side of the boulders that hid part of the beach from view and included a small secluded cove that few people knew about.

Max asked Quinn if she and Ashley could stop by the shop on Tuesday so she could pin up the hems of their gowns. "Bring the shoes you're wearing so I can get the length just right," she suggested.

"I'm sure Tuesday will work. I'll check with Ashley to make sure."

"Where'd she go?" Max looked around, but didn't see Ashley on the veranda. "She was just here."

"I think she went for a walk," Quinn said. "She tends to get restless. I've gotten used to her wandering off." She walked halfway down the steps scanning the beach. Was she looking for Ashley or her husband? Max wondered if Quinn felt uncomfortable with Gabby being alone with Nicholas after all.

"Are we in for some drama tonight?" Max quietly asked Olivia, wanting to be prepared for what might happen.

Olivia opened her mouth to answer when Nicholas returned, climbing the steps with Quinn behind him. He panted, out of breath by the time he reached the top step and joined them on the veranda. He and Gabby had made up he told them, but she wanted to stay on the beach and wait for the sunset.

"Should I join her?" Olivia asked. "I don't think she came all this way just to sit on the beach by herself."

"She really wants to be alone. I think all the excitement was a bit much for her. She acts so tough, but in many ways, she's really very fragile."

"I think I'm going to lie down for a bit," Quinn said, and Nicholas followed her inside. When he returned he told them, "I think the eight-hour car ride wore her out."

"I'm going to go look for Ashley," Olivia said. "I always get the feeling she feels like a third wheel. I wonder if that's why she's wandered off. I'll check on Gabby, too."

Ashley reappeared shortly after Olivia left and poured herself another glass of wine. She had taken a walk through the neighborhood instead of the beach, so she hadn't seen Olivia or Gabby.

"It's a charming town," Ashley said. "Such cute bungalows and I've never seen so many flowers in one place."

"We do love our gardens," Max agreed. "And since most of the homes don't have much of a back yard, if any, we do our gardening out front."

"Is everyone always so friendly?"

"Pretty much." Max smiled. She loved her little town.

Together Nicholas, Ashley and Max watched the sun slowly sink toward the horizon. Soon, the sky glowed in oranges and purples as the sun set, but Max, who lived in Crystal Shores and could see sunsets over the ocean nearly any night she wanted, seemed to be the only one paying attention. Nicholas still had on his sunglasses, which reflected the colors of the sunset, so as far as Max knew he could be asleep. Ashley stared at her phone, not looking up at all.

"I guess Olivia and Gabby are enjoying the sunset from the beach. Olivia's been gone nearly half an hour," Max said to no one in particular.

Max heard a faraway sound and got chills up and down her arms that had nothing to do with the cool sea air. It was a woman's scream.

CHAPTER FIVE

Max took off at a run, frustrated that she couldn't run faster on the soft sand in her strappy sandals. She headed for the boulders near the south side of the beach, not sure where the scream had come from. As she reached the shore, the waves receded leaving a wet piece of fabric in their wake. She walked over and picked up the blue gingham sash from Gabby's dress. Was it Gabby who had screamed?

Heading for the hidden cove, she rounded the largest boulder and came upon Olivia. Her friend stood with her hands over her mouth, her eyes wide.

"What's wrong?" Max grabbed Olivia's arm. "Was that you screaming?"

Olivia just stared at Gabby who lay sleeping on the beach towel. "She's dead," she said in barely more than a whisper.

Max ran to Gabby's side and checked her pulse, but felt nothing. There were red marks on her neck and Max looked at the sash she was still holding. She dropped it onto the sand. Was it the murder weapon?

"Do you have your phone?" she asked Olivia. Max had rushed off without hers.

Olivia handed Max her phone and she called 9-1-1. When the dispatcher got on the line, she calmly told him there was a dead body on the beach. She gave their location and tried to convince the man on the phone she'd already checked vital signs. She couldn't seem to convince him, so she followed his instructions, checking again for a pulse and breathing.

"Put the phone on speaker," Olivia said, seeming to regain some of her composure. "I took a CPR class last summer."

Max paced while Olivia performed CPR on Gabby's body, but Max was convinced it was pointless. She wished she had her own phone so she could call Detective Cruz and tell him her suspicions. A siren began to wail in the distance and Max walked toward the road to meet the paramedics. She looked up and down the beach, but whoever had killed Gabby would be long gone by now. She saw the ambulance pull up and waved to the driver, then returned to Olivia. She didn't want to leave her alone longer than she had to. The paramedics joined them moments later and took over. After several minutes, they stopped working. They didn't say anything to Max and Olivia, but Max knew that they had determined that Gabby was dead.

"Was it murder?" Olivia asked Max.

"Pretty sure it was," Max said.

"Who could have done this?"

Max only shook her head. She heard a gasp behind her and turned to see Ashley standing still, her eyes wide. She looked at Gabby's motionless body and the two paramedics. "Gabby?" Her voice quivered.

Nicholas hurried to her side. Ashley buried her head in his chest while he looked questioningly from Max to Olivia. "What happened?" he asked.

"She's dead," Olivia whispered. "We don't know what happened."

Quinn arrived and Ashley quickly pulled away from Nicholas. Quinn ran to Gabby's side, but Max grabbed her arm to keep her away from Gabby's body.

"Don't touch anything," Max said. "I'll wait for the police. Why don't you take Olivia back to the house? I think she's in shock."

"C'mon, Olivia," Quinn said, putting her arm around her friend's shoulder.

"Was it alcohol poisoning?" Nicholas asked. "She did have a lot to drink."

Max looked at Olivia and shook her head slightly. She didn't want Olivia to tell her friends that Max suspected murder. Not yet.

"Get back everyone," came a booming voice that Max immediately recognized. Her heart seemed to skip a beat just the way it did every time she saw him. Of course Detective Cruz was there. Part of her felt like everyone would be okay now. Except for Gabby. And except for the murderer.

oOo

Detective Cruz instructed the uniformed officer, Officer Daniels, to take everyone back to the beach house while he processed the crime scene.

"Where is CSI?" Max asked Jason. "And how did you get here so quickly?"

"CSI is on their way," he said. "I was on my way to dinner when I got the call."

The way he was dressed, he was apparently headed to a very nice restaurant. He wore a dark gray suit with an artistic looking tie, her favorite shade of royal blue. She figured this was not an appropriate time to compliment him on his choice of tie. His broad shoulders and trim waist were accentuated by the fit of the suit. There'd just been a murder. Why was she thinking of how good Jason looked in his suit? Olivia wasn't the only one in shock.

"Are you alright?" he asked. "You look dazed. It must be a shock seeing another dead body."

"I'm worried about Olivia," she said, her voice unsteady.

"I'm worried about you," he said. "And Olivia, too, of course."

"I made sure no one touched anything. I just touched her wrist to check for a pulse and Olivia performed CPR. Oh!" She remembered the sash. "I found the sash on the beach and picked it up while I was looking to see who'd screamed. I suppose the murderer dropped it. It seems careless, doesn't it?"

"If it was a crime of passion, they might not have been in their right mind," Detective Cruz said. "They could have walked away with the sash and then just dropped it when they realized they were still holding it."

"Can you get prints off of fabric?" Max asked.

"It's possible. Not an easy process. And there'll be your fingerprints and Gabby's on it."

"And probably Olivia's. It was her dress." Max stared at Gabby's body. "You'd think I'd be used to seeing dead bodies by now. Do you ever get used to it?"

"No," he admitted. "Why don't you go in the house with everyone else. I'll be in as soon as we finish processing the crime scene." He reached out and touched her arm, and before Max knew what she was doing, she buried her face in his chest. His strong arms held her close and he gently stroked her hair. For a moment, she forgot where they were. She forgot he had a girlfriend.

Max stepped back, feeling embarrassed. "I'm sorry your date was ruined."

"My date!" His eyes got wide and he ran back in the direction of the street where his car must have been parked. Had he really left Lori waiting for him and forgotten all about her?

Max headed back to the house, trudging back through the sand and climbing the steps to the deserted veranda. She found the friends sprawled on the sofa and armchairs in the living room looking forlorn and not saying a word.

Who killed Gabby? She looked at each one of Olivia's friends. Could one of them have strangled their friend? Gabby was petite and drunk. How much strength would it have taken?

"I'm going to get something to drink," Max said, but walked past the kitchen and down the hall to the bedrooms. The beds in all three rooms looked freshly made without a wrinkle on the comforters. None of them looked like someone had been lying down on them. One of the rooms had an armchair. Maybe Quinn had been reading or checking emails or something. But why had she said she was going to lie down?

Max shook her head. She'd become so suspicious of everyone lately, and she didn't like thinking that one of Olivia's friends could be a murderer. Next thing she knew, she'd be suspecting

Olivia. Grabbing a soda out of the refrigerator, she heard Nicholas mention seeing a man on the beach. Max rejoined the group in the living room.

"He looked kinda scruffy," he said, "like he hadn't shaved in a few days and he could have used a haircut. Did anyone else see him?"

"Yes, I saw him," said Ashley. "He looked like a homeless person."

"Oh, I don't know," Nicholas said. "The way he was dressed he didn't look homeless."

Officer Daniels spoke tentatively. "I don't think you should be talking about who you saw until Detective Cruz questions you."

They probably shouldn't be talking at all, but Officer Daniels was young and probably hadn't had a great deal of training on how to conduct a murder investigation. In spite of what had happened in the past year and a half, no one expected murders in their quiet town. Max remembered Officer Daniels from the Crystal Shores playhouse when she and Keiko had been sequestered with a group of actors. He had seemed tentative then, too.

"I thought this was a private beach," Nicholas said to no one in particular.

"It's not private," Max said, "but very few people come down this far. It's a bit of a walk from the main beach and you have to climb over a few boulders or wait for low tide so you can walk on the sand. In California, there are laws that allow the public access to the beach up to the high tide line."

"How egalitarian of the state," he said.

"You didn't grow up in California?"

"No, I grew up on Long Island. My parents never took us to the beach. I spent most of my childhood in the library."

"I loved the library when I was a kid. Still do," Max said, feeling a little sorry for him. She spent most of her summers in the ocean playing in the water and on the sand and couldn't imagine otherwise. "What genre do you like to read?"

"I used to read pretty much everything," Nicholas said.

"But now you hardly ever read," Ashley said. "You guys hardly have any books in your house."

"I have other hobbies," he said. Max wondered what they were besides drinking.

The group was quiet again until Olivia spoke. "Gabby was a lot of fun when we were kids," she reminisced. "She used to come to my house all the time. My mom fed her whenever she'd come over. I don't think she ate much besides canned spaghetti and cereal at home."

"She was fun in college, too," Quinn said. "She just never knew when enough was enough. And her taste in men was atrocious." She realized her faux pas, and added, "Sorry, dear."

"No apology necessary," he said. "I didn't really know her, just… I mean, we really only hung out a couple of times."

"Don't worry. You don't have to go into detail," Quinn assured him. "In fact, please don't."

"Well, I thought she was a pain," Ashley said.

"Ashley!" Quinn exclaimed, sounding shocked.

"Well, she was. When we were in college, the only time she showed up was when she either needed a place to stay or wanted to borrow money. How much did she borrow from you Quinn?"

"It doesn't really matter now. Poor thing." Quinn ran her hand through her short, dark hair and shook her head sadly. "She never really had a chance, and now she's dead. We'll never know if she would have turned her life around."

Max had thought Gabby had been a bit of a free spirit, but now it sounded like she had real issues. "What kind of problems did she have? I'm guessing by tonight that alcohol was one of them."

"And drugs," Ashley said.

"You don't know that," Olivia said. "I mean some pot, sure, but you don't know that she did any hard drugs."

"Hello," Ashley said. "Earth to Olivia. Reality is calling. You're in denial if you think she wasn't doing coke or meth. Or worse."

"Any chance she'd found a dealer in town?" Max asked.

Everyone looked at her and stared. Everyone except Olivia who explained to her friends that Max had helped solve two murders in town.

"Two murders?" Quinn said, dumbfounded. "What kind of town is this?"

CHAPTER SIX

There was a knock on the sliding glass door that led to the veranda. "So, who's the handsome detective?" Ashley asked as Max went to open the door.

"Hands off. He belongs to Max," Olivia said.

Max turned to look at Olivia in surprise at this comment and ran right into the glass door. "Ow," she said, trying to hide her embarrassment. She slid the door open and Jason motioned her to come outside.

Max sat down in a cushioned patio chair. She blinked at the bright lights on the veranda and shivered in the cool ocean breeze. She rubbed her arms to warm them. For once she didn't have her favorite sweater with her, thanks to Keiko. A hundred feet away, the waves crashed against the shore, the whitecaps glowing in the light of a nearly full moon.

Detective Cruz took off his jacket and put it around her shoulders even though she protested she was fine.

"Another murder?" the detective said disapprovingly. "Are you going for some kind of a record?"

"It's not my fault. If it's anyone's fault, it's yours. You're the one who's supposed to keep law and order in this town."

"Okay, it's nobody's fault. Just tell me what happened."

Max told him everything she remembered from the time Gabby arrived in town. She included the argument Keiko overheard between Nicholas and Gabby. The detective wrote everything in his little notebook without any noticeable reaction.

"Nicholas was the last one to see her alive," she concluded. "Well, as far as I know. Ashley was out for a walk at the time, but hadn't mentioned seeing Gabby. He was only gone maybe five, ten minutes."

"But you're not sure what time that was?" he asked.

"No." Max hadn't been paying attention to the time. "I would guess it was around an hour before Olivia found her body. Let me think." She tried hard to remember. "Maybe it was less than an hour, but it was definitely more than a half hour. Maybe forty-five minutes."

"So, when Nicholas went to talk to Gabby, Ashley was out taking a walk and Quinn went to lie down as soon as Nicholas returned." He looked up from his notebook. "Did anyone check on Quinn?"

"No. I didn't see her again until they all came down to the beach after we all heard Olivia scream."

"And Olivia was gone about a half hour before you heard her scream?"

"Yes, she left right after Nicholas came back. She went looking for Ashley."

"Who came back right after Olivia left."

"Yes." Max stared at him, wanting to know what he was thinking. "You can't really think it was any of them, do you?" She didn't want to tell him she had been wondering if one of them could be a killer. "What possible motive would they have? They haven't seen her in years. Don't you think it's more likely that a stranger surprised her on the beach and stole her ring? It's an emerald so it must have been very valuable. Nicholas and Ashley saw someone on the beach."

"Oh, really?" His eyebrows rose almost imperceptibly. "And why were you discussing this when you knew I was going to question everyone in the house?"

Max ignored his question. "She was strangled, wasn't she?" Max asked.

The detective's eyes narrowed. "We'll know more after the autopsy. Until then, it's best if you let the police handle it."

"Oh, of course. I was just wondering, because it seems like she would have screamed at the very least if a stranger attacked her."

"That is puzzling," he said staring at his notebook for a moment, then looking up at her. "I gather she had a lot to drink. If she were passed out, it would be much easier to surprise her and strangle her before she could scream. Do you know how much she had to drink?"

"A lot," she said. "At least three or four drinks. Is that enough to make her pass out?"

"Three or four shots is a lot of alcohol for someone her size, but I have a feeling no one was measuring shots precisely. We'll know her blood alcohol level soon." He stared at his notebook for a moment as if something was bothering him. "If she was passed out, why would someone walk up to an unconscious woman and strangle her?" He made some more scribbles then looked up. "I need to question everyone and take a good hard look at the evidence. That's how you solve a case."

"Right," Max said, thinking she wouldn't mind taking a look at the evidence.

He hesitated as if he had something to say that he didn't want to tell her. "I hate to tell you this, but Olivia's a suspect, too."

"What? But she's the one who found the body. And I'm betting that the time of death wasn't just before I called 9-1-1."

"But according to your timeline, Olivia left the house at least half an hour before you called 9-1-1 at eight twenty-seven. She and Ashley don't have an alibi, and Quinn's alibi is that she was sleeping in another room, which isn't exactly iron clad as far as alibis go. Nicholas says Gabby was still alive when he saw her, but we only have his word for it. Our preliminary determination of time of death is between seven and eight o'clock, so I have to consider all your friends as suspects."

"You mean Olivia's friends," she corrected him. "You know Olivia. You can't possibly think she killed her friend right before her wedding day."

"Of course I don't. But it doesn't matter what I think. This is a murder investigation and she doesn't have an alibi."

"Well, you'd better hurry up and eliminate Olivia from your suspect list, or I can't be your friend any longer." She turned and walked back into the house without another word.

oOo

Detective Cruz took Quinn out onto the veranda next to question. He was a very methodical detective, and as angry as Max was that he considered her friend a suspect, she had confidence that he would find out who really murdered Gabby. And she would help find the truth even if he didn't want her involved.

Officer Daniels stood at attention while they sat in the living room awkwardly making small talk. What did you talk about when someone you knew had just been killed? The murder had been sobering, but Nicholas seemed determined to fix that by mixing another pitcher of martinis. Olivia, who had to drive home after Detective Cruz was done with them, drank a diet soda.

Olivia was next to be questioned, and Max waited nervously, staring at the door which led out to the veranda wondering how their conversation was going. Was Detective Cruz telling Olivia she was a suspect?

"So, you and the detective, huh?" Ashley said and Max turned around to look at her. Max didn't care for her tone of voice.

"We're just friends," Max said. She didn't bother to mention he had a girlfriend. It was none of her business, after all.

"Then you don't mind…" Ashley began.

"Ashley!" Quinn snapped at her. "Have some decency. Our friend just died."

"Decency? How about being decent enough to admit that she was not our friend? Maybe she was still Olivia's friend, but if so, Olivia's the most tolerant person I know. She screwed all of us over in one way or another. You know it's true."

Max was curious. "You mean like borrowing money and not paying it back?"

Ashley looked at Quinn before she answered. "Yeah. She was a mooch." Max was sure there was more to the story than that, but decided not to pry further. She'd ask Olivia later.

Ashley didn't have an alibi for the time of the murder. She claimed to be walking around the neighborhood, but they only had her word for that. Had she actually gone down to the beach to see Gabby? Did Ashley have a reason to want her dead?

oOo

Max insisted on spending the night with Olivia, who was visibly upset, and no wonder. Her childhood friend had been murdered. It was never easy when someone you knew died, but this was a shock that would take some time to get over. Not to mention, one of her other friends might be the culprit. Max hoped this wouldn't put a damper on Olivia's wedding, but she couldn't see how it wouldn't. The wedding was just a week away. That was hardly enough time to grieve and mourn a friend.

It was almost midnight when they arrived at Olivia's little two-bedroom cottage on Aster Street. Olivia unlocked the red-painted front door and they stepped into her cozy living room, which contained an off-white overstuffed sofa covered in pillows and a floral print easy chair. Art Deco posters hung on the wall, and family photographs covered the mantelpiece over the fireplace.

"Do you think it's too late to call Zach?" Olivia asked. "He's probably asleep."

"I think he'd be upset if you didn't call him."

"You're probably right." She went into the bedroom and Max heard the two of them talking though she couldn't hear the words. She could tell Olivia was crying.

Max pulled out her phone to call her dad and let him know where she was in case he heard about the murder. She didn't want him worrying about her. Before she had a chance to call, her phone rang and he was calling her.

"Fiona just called me and said one of Olivia's friends was dead," he said.

"Fiona? How did she know? Oh, never mind. Nothing happens in this town that she doesn't know about." Fiona McNulty owned the Knitpickers yarn store next door to Wedding Belles. She was as nosy as she was kind and generous, which is to say very. It was rumored that she was the ringleader of a telephone hotline, and every time something happened in Crystal Shores she got a call. And once Fiona got a call, it wasn't long before everyone in town knew.

"When did you get in on the gossip hotline?" she asked.

"It's not gossip." He sounded slightly offended. "It's important information. I'm part of the neighborhood watch."

"If you say so," Max said. "I'll tell you everything in the morning. I'm staying with Olivia tonight."

"Be safe, okay?" he said.

"Of course, Dad. Love you."

Max dug through her purse until she found the notepad she always carried with her. It was tiny, but it would have to do. She wrote down everything she remembered about the evening, but it didn't help her make sense of the murder.

Olivia finally came out of her bedroom, her eyes red. "I feel better. Zach said to thank you for staying with me." She handed Max a t-shirt and yoga pants to sleep in. While Max changed, Olivia fixed two mugs of chamomile tea. Max let her friend have some quiet time while they both let the day's events sink in.

Olivia finally spoke. "I can't believe she's gone and I'll never see her again."

"When was the last time you'd seen her? I mean before she showed up in town today?" Max breathed in the warm, fragrant steam of the chamomile tea.

"Last Christmas when I went home to see my parents. She had just come out of rehab."

Max looked at Olivia with surprise. "So, she did have a drug problem."

"I don't know." She shook her head sadly. "It was alcohol or drugs. She never told me and I didn't ask. I didn't want to say anything to the others. I don't like them saying bad things about her, especially now."

"You cared about her." Max put her tea down and reached out for Olivia's hand, giving it a gentle squeeze. She wished there were more she could do.

"Gabby was a free spirit, like a child almost. In some ways, she was very innocent. She had it rough growing up. Her father wasn't around at all and her mother was only there physically. She was too self-involved to be a good mother. My mother could only do so much. She'd feed her when she came over and was always giving her my old clothes, even some that I wasn't ready to get rid of." A smile briefly appeared on Olivia's face but quickly faded.

"Sounds like she was really lucky to have you for a friend," Max said.

"Lucky? Being my friend got her killed! She wouldn't have been anywhere near Crystal Shores if it weren't for me. It's my fault she's dead."

"Don't say that, Olivia." Max hoped this was just the grief and shock talking and Olivia wouldn't carry the guilt over Gabby's death with her for years to come. That would be a terrible burden. "Gabby came here because she wanted to be with you when you got married. She was so happy to surprise you, almost like she was pulling a prank on you."

Olivia sighed. "She always did like a good prank. I think April Fool's Day was her favorite holiday. Maybe that was because she didn't get a lot of gifts at Christmas or her birthday. On April Fool's, she was the one in control, and she made sure everyone got something unexpected." Olivia leaned back on the pillows and sighed. "I'm suddenly exhausted."

"I'm not surprised," Max said. She could hardly keep her eyes open, but she'd stay up all night if that's what Olivia needed.

"Do you think a stranger killed her?" Olivia asked. "It must have been a stranger," she said, answering her own question. "I think Detective Cruz suspects my friends. But I know them. They couldn't possibly have done something like this."

"I'm sure we'll know more soon," Max said. She didn't want to upset Olivia by telling her that she suspected her friends, too. The idea of a stranger strangling her to steal a ring seemed far-fetched.

Olivia brought out sheets and blankets for the sofa and helped Max make it into a bed, since the second bedroom was being used for storing Zach's belongings. He planned to move in after the honeymoon. Olivia said goodnight, and then stopped and turned around on the way to her room. "I've never been a murder suspect before. It's a bit disconcerting."

"Just about everyone is a suspect," Max said.

"It was lucky that you stayed in the house while we were all wandering about. Can you imagine how awkward it would be if Detective Cruz had you on his suspect list?"

"Hopefully they'll find out who did it soon." Even Max, as suspicious as she was at times, found it hard to believe that Nicholas, Quinn or Ashley were murderers.

"I wish Zach were here. Or my mom and dad." Olivia smiled at Max. "Thank you for staying with me. I really needed someone to talk to. And I feel safer with you here."

"Zach gets back on Wednesday, right?"

"Yes. Then he's off work for two and a half weeks." Olivia's smile faded. "I need to know who did it," she said, with a determined sound in her voice. "I won't have any peace until I find out."

"Don't worry," Max said, reassuring her friend. "Detective Cruz will figure it out."

"With your help, of course." Olivia gave Max a hug and turned to head to her room.

"Can I ask you something before you go to bed?" Max hesitated even when Olivia nodded. But she needed to know. "What did Gabby do to make Ashley so angry?"

"Oh, I don't know," Olivia said. "Lots of stuff, probably. I think she stole away one of Ashley's boyfriends, but I don't think she was that into him anyway. Maybe Gabby just lied to her one too many times. Ashley will give you the shirt off her back, but if you betray her trust, well, let's just say that she can hold a grudge."

"That's interesting," Max whispered to herself after Olivia closed the door. She had promised herself to stay out of police business after the last murder was solved. Of course, it didn't occur to her then that there would be another murder in their little town or that Olivia would be considered a suspect.

Tomorrow she'd start by talking to the three friends. The sooner she cleared them of suspicion, the sooner they could find the real murderer. Of course, that was assuming that one of them didn't kill Gabby. She'd learned that murders were rarely random.

CHAPTER SEVEN

When Max awoke, for a moment she didn't know where she was. The memory of yesterday's incidents came flooding back and along with them her determination to help find out who murdered Gabby. It was only six, which was earlier than she usually got up, especially on a Sunday, but she had plans for the day. She dressed and left Olivia a note. This morning, she really wanted to talk to Detective Cruz. She didn't know if he would be going for a jog on the beach today, but it was her best chance to talk to him alone. She had to convince him that Olivia wasn't capable of murder. And maybe if she caught him when he was off duty, he'd be more likely to share what he knew.

The walk home took her twenty minutes, walking briskly past colorful cottages, white picket fences, and beautifully tended flowerbeds. On a normal day, she would stop to smell the roses along the way, but this wasn't a normal day. The sky was gray and overcast, which matched her mood.

After stopping home for a quick shower and change of clothes, Max walked the two blocks to the beach and took off her sandals so her feet could sink into the cool sand. She felt the tension in her shoulders relax as she listened to the waves crashing against the shore and breathed in the damp, salty air. The ocean always had that effect on her. Looking up and down the beach she saw a few people out for a morning walk or jog, but there was no sign of the detective. The sun peeked through the clouds, the light glistening on the water. Seagulls cried out overhead and a few sandpipers darted in and out of the waves.

Max smiled in spite of herself as her dark mood floated away with the clouds. Out of habit, she began to look among the pebbles in the wet sand searching for the telltale glint of sea glass. She had a few blue pieces at home that she could give Olivia if she needed something blue. Her gown had pockets, like all the gowns Max designed, and brides were always grateful to have a place to keep a lipstick or tissue. Olivia could put a piece of blue sea glass in one of hers. Did she need something old? Was that her responsibility as maid of honor, or would Olivia's mother be giving her something? Olivia's parents arrived on Wednesday, so she could ask her mother then. Max had a pair of pearl earrings that were once her grandmother's she could loan the bride. Maybe she should have thought of this sooner.

A tap on her shoulder made her jump and she twirled around, her hands up ready to ward off the attacker.

"Whoa," Detective Cruz said. "Don't hurt me."

Max gave him a sheepish grin. "I'm just a little on edge."

Detective Cruz apologized for startling her.

"I wasn't sure you'd be here this morning," Max said, "but I'm glad you are. I hope you've crossed Olivia off your suspect list."

"I haven't had a chance to do anything besides process the crime scene, transcribe my notes, and get in a little sleep." He seemed to react to the determined stare she was giving him. "I'll make sure I clear Olivia as soon as I can," he said gently.

"Thank you," she said, softening. He was a good detective, so she didn't know why she was so worried. He'd find out who murdered Gabby, and she'd help in any way she could.

"Besides," he said wearily, "I don't need to give you any reasons to interfere with the investigation."

"Interfere?" Her voice rose with the outrage she felt. "If I hadn't interfered in the past, there might be two murderers running around free in this town."

"So now you're a detective?"

"That's not the point."

"So what is the point?" he asked, crossing his arms over his chest.

"The point is, I'm not going to stay out of your investigation when you're considering my best friend as one of your prime suspects."

"I never said she was a prime suspect. If you will let me do my job I can solve this case and in doing so, clear Olivia's name."

"Since when am I not letting you do your job?" Max demanded to know.

"Just stay out of it this time," he said, and turned and walked away before she could say anything else.

It took a while for her anger to subside, and then Max realized she'd missed her opportunity to find out if he'd learned anything. She wasn't sure why she was so angry. She knew from experience that the police didn't like civilians getting involved in police work, but he'd been open to at least listening to her before. What was different now? With his current attitude, it seemed unlikely that he would share his information with her. How was she going to solve the murder if he wouldn't tell her what he knew? It was like trying to put together a jigsaw puzzle blindfolded.

oOo

Max unlocked the back door of her dad's house and stepped into his kitchen. She breathed in the welcome scent of fresh brewed coffee. Richard Walters set up the coffee and oatmeal the night before so it was ready for both of them in the morning. She didn't have an appetite this particular morning, so she poured a cup of coffee, added cream and sugar, and sat down at the dining table to think.

Max was the only one at the beach house last night who had an ironclad alibi. Good thing, she thought ruefully, or Detective Cruz would have put her on his suspect list. Was it possible one of Olivia's friends could be a murderer?

She thought back to Nicholas walking up the steps to the veranda after he'd gone to talk to Gabby. Could he have been lying about her being alive when he saw her? At the time, he seemed to have the same bored attitude he'd had all evening. Was it possible he'd strangled Gabby and then just sauntered up the stairs to rejoin them?

Ashley didn't hide her dislike of Gabby. But her issues with the dead woman seemed petty—nothing more than unpaid loans and stolen boyfriends. Not anything to kill over. Besides, none of Olivia's friends had seen Gabby since college. That was a long time to hold a grudge, but she remembered a phrase she'd heard once: Revenge is a dish best served cold.

"Good morning, sunshine." Her father's voice interrupted her thoughts.

"Morning, Dad," Max answered.

"Is Olivia okay?" Richard asked. "She must be devastated."

As if on cue, Max's phone buzzed with a text from Olivia.

Wedding is off

Max sighed. Some things should not be communicated via text message. She called Olivia.

"What do you mean the wedding's off?" Max asked. "I thought you were going to wait until Zach got home."

Richard's eyebrows rose.

"I talked to him this morning and he agreed," Olivia said.

"You mean you talked him into it. I bet he's not happy about it. Why don't you just wait a few days? I'll come by later and we can talk about it."

Max hung up the phone and slumped in her chair. Olivia had done so much work planning the wedding, and Max knew Olivia couldn't wait to marry Zach. She was worried about her friend. Her dream wedding had turned into a nightmare.

There was a knock on the back door and Richard and Max looked at each other.

"Expecting someone?" Richard asked.

Max shook her head and got up to answer the door. Keiko stood there with a big smile. She wore a pink Hello Kitty t-shirt, wide-legged pink and white striped pants, and pink tennis shoes. A pink beret topped her shoulder length hair.

"Hi!" Max motioned for Keiko to come in. "What's up?"

"What do you mean, 'what's up?'"

Max was perplexed. "What do you mean, 'what do I mean?'"

"It's Sunday," Keiko prompted.

"Oh!" Max exclaimed, as she remembered why Keiko was there. "We're supposed to have brunch together."

"You forgot?" Keiko asked. "That's not like you. Is this a bad time?"

"You haven't heard. Sit down and I'll tell you both everything."

She was halfway through her story when her dad asked, "Nicholas Buckley? The guy who wrote *Immersion?*"

"Yeah. It's a trilogy."

"I know. I've only read the first one. It's a real page turner. The sea level has risen and all the rich people have bought up all the higher ground. Everyone else has to try to survive on what little land is left."

"I read it in high school," Keiko said. "Pretty much everyone I knew read the whole trilogy."

Richard said, "It's not what I usually read but I kept hearing about it so I thought I'd read it."

"What I don't understand is why he's never written anything else," Max said.

"He's not the first author to quit writing after having a huge success," Richard said. "Maybe it's just hard to know how to follow up on it."

"Maybe," Max said. She couldn't help wondering if there were more to it.

CHAPTER EIGHT

Rose Street Cafe had the best poached eggs on toast. Max didn't know what made them so good, she just accepted the fact. She and Keiko sat on the patio with their cappuccinos and waited for their food to arrive.

"We need to go shopping and get you a new sweater," Keiko said with a scowl.

"But I just got this one the last time we went shopping," Max protested. "I love it." The tan sweater was as soft as a cuddly blanket. And, since Keiko had helped pick it out, it was very stylish and fit beautifully.

"I'm glad you like it," Keiko said, the smile returning to her face. "But that was a year ago. You have worn that sweater nearly every day since you bought it. It's time."

"Has it really been a year? I'd love to go shopping with you, but I'm not throwing out this one like you made me do with my last sweater."

Keiko laughed. "You may keep this one. But I don't want to see it anymore."

"Agreed. By the way, where did you go last night that was so important?"

"I was just meeting a friend. Now about this murder." Keiko changed the subject and became serious. "I will research all the suspects. Except not Olivia, of course. What do you need to know?"

"Everything," Max said. "Detective Cruz doesn't seem willing to tell me anything. I don't know why he's being so stubborn."

"What happened to calling him Jason?"

"Jason is my friend's name. Detective Cruz is the cop. Right now, he's not my friend."

"I see." Keiko looked disappointed. "But it doesn't matter. You have me, after all. What would you like to know?"

"If a stranger murdered her, they would be long gone by now, wouldn't they?"

"Not necessarily," Keiko said. "If it was someone who lived around here, then skipping town would make them look guilty. If they thought they had gotten away with it, then they might just stay put."

Max gave this some thought. "Then it would be good to know who in town has a criminal record. Is that information accessible to the public?"

"I can see what I can find out. I am very resourceful."

Max smiled. That was an understatement. "I know so little about Olivia's friends." She stirred her cappuccino, wondering if one of them could possibly be a murderer. "Maybe they have secrets."

"Everyone has secrets," Keiko said.

"Even you?" Max raised her eyebrows.

Keiko laughed nervously. "Oh no. Not me. I have no secrets."

Max eyed her skeptically, but let it go. "Is there any way for you to find out if there have been reports of criminal activity in the area? I mean, legally."

Keiko sighed. "Do you really want to play by the rules? When Detective Cruz isn't giving you the information you need?"

"Yes, Keiko. I want you to play by the rules." The last thing she wanted was for Keiko to get in trouble trying to help her. "I'll get him to talk to me one way or the other. I need to know what he knows."

"You will use your feminine wiles?" Keiko asked.

"My what? No, I'm just going to appeal to his sense of logic and fairness. And explain that he needs my help."

"I would go for the wiles if I were you."

Their poached eggs arrived, and they were quiet as they ate, each lost in their own thoughts.

If a stranger had killed Gabby, then Detective Cruz was the one to find out who did it. But if one of Olivia's friends was a murderer, Max knew she had an edge on the detective. She could find out more than he ever would. People let their guard down around her the way they never would with the police.

She needed to spend more time with Nicholas, Quinn, and Ashley. Now, how to go about it?

oOo

After her late brunch, Max wouldn't be hungry until dinnertime, but she guessed that Olivia had eaten little or nothing. She ate like a bird as it was, and it was important to eat well in stressful times. Max ordered Olivia's favorite veggie burger and two iced teas to go.

She found Olivia red-faced from crying.

"I don't know what's wrong with me," Olivia said. "I can't stop crying. I keep seeing her lying there."

Max tried to console Olivia. "She was your friend. Of course you're upset. Now that the shock has worn off, you have to deal with your grief."

"Then I start worrying about the wedding and then I feel guilty and selfish. Gabby will never have the chance to get married."

"That doesn't mean that you shouldn't have the chance."

"It's this Saturday," Olivia said. "If we're going to cancel it, we need to do it soon."

"But not right now," Max said. "What did Zach say?"

"He said to wait until he gets home on Wednesday." Olivia leaned back on the sofa, crossing her arms over her chest. She blinked back tears that threatened to return.

"So it's settled. I don't want you to worry about it any more until then." Max hoped that Zach would be able to talk her out of it. If anyone could, he was the one to do it.

Olivia protested but finally acquiesced. The two women moved to the dining room table with their iced teas, and Olivia daintily nibbled at the veggie burger.

Olivia's phone rang, and she glanced at the display but didn't answer it. Then the texts started on both their phones. Fiona's gossip hotline had done its work, and Max suspected their friends and neighbors were hoping to get more details. On a positive note, everyone who texted seemed concerned about Olivia and wanted to know if she was okay.

Max took Olivia's phone away from her and scanned through the texts until she came upon one from Olivia's mother.

"Do you want me to talk to her and tell her what's happened?" Max looked at the text. The gossip hadn't reached all the way to New Jersey where Olivia's parents lived. "I can give her a call if you're not up to it."

"No, right now I want my mommy. I wish she were here already." She took the phone from Max and as soon as the call was answered, she started crying. "Gabby's dead, Mom. I saw her. It was horrible."

Max could only imagine what it was like to see your childhood friend killed so brutally. She went into the bathroom and brought back a box of tissues, then went into the bedroom so Olivia could have some privacy. She took her purse with her so she could check her own messages, and there were plenty.

Then she noticed a message from Quinn.

We're all worried about Olivia. She's not answering my calls or texts. Let us know how she's doing.

Max texted that Olivia was doing as well as could be expected.

Quinn seemed to be satisfied with that answer. Then she saw a text from Zach who was trying to get an early flight back. All the flights were full, so he was at the airport waiting to get a seat on any plane coming to southern California. Zach asked Max not to tell Olivia in case he wasn't able to get home early. He didn't want to get her hopes up.

Max peeked into the other room and Olivia was still on the phone with her mother so she went back into the bedroom. Max could completely relate. Every time something happened she wished she still had her mom around to talk to. Her dad was the best, but there were times you just wanted to talk to your mom.

Olivia came in the bedroom and sat down next to her on the bed.

"Feeling better?" Max could tell with one look that she was.

Olivia managed a weak smile. "I told her not to come since we might cancel the wedding, but she insisted that she's coming either way."

"Your dad, too?"

Olivia nodded. "I'm really glad they didn't listen to me. They'll be here on Wednesday."

"Good. And Zach gets home on Wednesday, too. Until then, you have me."

"I miss Zach so much." Olivia got up from the bed. "I feel lost without him. How do you get so dependent on someone in just one year?" She scrunched her face. "Dependent isn't the right word. I just feel safe with him around. He always knows what I need to hear."

"He's a great guy," Max said, thinking that sounded lame. "And you're in love."

"Head over heels," Olivia said, finally smiling. She took her mostly uneaten lunch and put it in the refrigerator. "How about we watch one of those old movies you love?"

"*I* love?" Max grinned, happy that her friend seemed to be recovering from her slump. "You're the one who owns them all.

I just come over for the popcorn." She followed Olivia back out to the living room.

"Right. By the way, I let Zach know that you and I will still be having movie night after we're married. He said he wouldn't have it any other way. His only condition is that I make enough popcorn for the three of us. I hope to be making popcorn for four sometime soon."

"Four?" Max wondered what she meant. Babies don't eat popcorn. Then she got it. "I don't know about that. I'm not sure I'm ready for anything serious."

"I think Detective Jason Cruz might be ready for something serious," Olivia teased.

"Him? He can go jump in the lake. Besides, he has a girlfriend."

"Oh, I wouldn't worry too much about her," Olivia said in a knowing voice.

"So you've met her?" Max folded her arms across her chest. Olivia was the one person who knew about her crush on the detective. "Why didn't you tell me?"

"I met her once. I don't think it's anything serious. Besides, she's not his type."

"Not his type? She's every guy's type. Tall, blond, and gorgeous. Anyway, I don't want to talk about him or his girlfriend." She also didn't want to talk about Olivia being a suspect, which was part of the reason she was mad at him.

"Did you two have a falling out?" Olivia asked. "I hope it wasn't over me."

"Over you?" Max grabbed the remote and turned the TV on. "What are you talking about?" She tried to sound innocent, but wasn't sure she succeeded.

"I know I'm a suspect, Max." She grabbed the remote from Max and sat down on the sofa, pulling Max down next to her. "Think about it. What kind of a detective would he be if he didn't consider me a suspect just because I'm your friend? I'll tell you. A lousy one."

"Well, it's not just because you're my friend. He knows you. He must know you couldn't have done it." Max sulked. She didn't want to forgive Jason just because it was the reasonable thing to do.

"And I'm sure he does. But you know how he is. He does things by the book, and it gets him very good results. He's solved two murders in town." Olivia searched through the movies available stopping at *The Big Sleep*.

"I helped a little."

"You helped a lot. The two of you make a good team. Don't let your emotions get the better of you."

"When have I ever… never mind. Are you making popcorn, or what?"

CHAPTER NINE

Olivia's phone rang a few more times, but since she didn't recognize the numbers she didn't answer it. Max figured she didn't want to have to talk to anyone about the murder right now. *The Big Sleep* was just the thing to get their minds off of it.

Humphrey Bogart had just kissed Lauren Bacall when there was a knock on the door. Olivia paused the movie and got up to answer it.

Max heard a male voice she recognized. "I was hoping we could talk."

"Come in, Detective Cruz," Olivia said, opening the door wider so he could enter.

Max cringed. She didn't want to see him yet. If she'd been quicker, she could have hidden in the bedroom.

"Hello Max," the detective said. "I'm glad you're here. I was hoping to talk to you, too."

"Hello," she mumbled. She knew Olivia was right, and he was just doing his job, but after the things she'd said she felt awkward being in the same room as him.

Olivia invited Detective Cruz to sit down on the armchair and sat back down on the sofa next to Max.

"Have you notified Gabby's father?" Olivia asked.

"We haven't been able to locate him. I was hoping you had a number."

"No," Olivia said. "I've never met him. He wasn't around when Gabby was a kid. They reconnected after her mother died."

"When was that?" Max wondered.

"A few years ago," Olivia said. "It was just before Gabby dropped out of college."

"I just have a few questions about last night," the detective began. He took his notebook out of his pocket.

Max had questions of her own. "It didn't look like there was a struggle. Did you find any evidence that there was?"

"No," he said. "But according to everyone who was there that night, she had a lot to drink. She may have been passed out when she was killed."

"What was her blood alcohol level?"

"I really can't release that information," he said.

"Can't? More like won't." She didn't know why he was so reluctant to tell her the details about the case. "If a stranger came along and wanted to steal her ring, wouldn't they have tried to grab it and only stabbed her if she fought back?"

"One would think, but criminals are not always logical. What's bothering me is how a stranger would just happen by and decide to steal a ring that didn't appear especially valuable. From the description I was given, it didn't sound like the stone was very large."

"It was an emerald," Olivia said. "About a carat set in platinum. She inherited it from her grandmother. She hocked it once and her dad had to get it back. He was really angry and didn't give it back for a long time, not until the last time she got out of rehab. I think he was hoping it was the last time. She told me she got a grand for it at the pawnshop, but I'm sure it was worth much more. But you're right. It wasn't flashy or gaudy. And I don't know how someone would know it was a real emerald just by looking at it. But someone must have known, since it's gone."

Detective Cruz wrote the information down.

"What's in the folder?" Max had wondered about it since he arrived.

"Nicholas and Ashley came down to the station and described the person they saw on the beach to a sketch artist." He took two sketches out of the folder and handed one to Max and one to Olivia. "Do you recognize this person?"

Max stared at the sketch in her hands. She took the other sketch from Olivia. "The two sketches don't look like the same person."

"I agree," Jason said. "They have the same shaggy hair and two-day growth, but other than that, there's little or no similarity."

"Maybe they didn't get a good look at him?" Max suggested. "I don't think it was likely there were two scruffy looking guys at the beach within a half hour. Or maybe they made him up."

"What?" Olivia said, sounding startled.

"I heard Nicholas mentioning someone with shaggy hair and stubbly beard and Ashley said she saw him, too. The shaggy hair and stubble is the only thing these two pictures have in common."

"Do either of them look familiar?" Jason asked.

Max stared at the two sketches. "This one looks vaguely familiar," she said, trying to remember where she'd seen the man. Detective Cruz and Olivia waited quietly. "I think I've seen him on the beach," she finally said. "He looked a little out of place because he was wearing jeans and it was a really hot afternoon. I think it was a week or two ago."

"Do you remember anything else?" Detective Cruz asked.

"No, he just seemed to be wandering aimlessly along the shore. I think he was barefoot, but he may have been carrying his shoes. That's all I can remember. I'm not even sure it's the same guy."

"What about you, Olivia?" the detective asked.

"I don't recognize either of them," Olivia said.

"Ashley said she didn't get a very good look at him," the detective said, "so it's possible they both saw the same person. I had Nicholas and Ashley look at mug shots, but they didn't see anyone who looked like the stranger they say they saw."

Max noticed he said "they say." Did he not believe them? The only reason for them to lie about seeing a stranger would be if they had something to do with Gabby's death.

"Olivia, I'm doing everything I can to get you off the suspect list." He leaned forward in his chair. "You understand, don't you?"

"Of course, Detective Cruz. I'm not worried. I just want you to find out who killed Gabby."

"Good." He sounded relieved and gave Max a pleading look, as if asking for forgiveness. "Now, if you don't mind, walk me through everything that happened yesterday evening one more time."

Max and Olivia recounted every detail about the evening, but they didn't remember anything they hadn't already told the detective the night before. Then Cruz asked Olivia to tell him about each one of her friends.

Nicholas had written the *Immersion* trilogy just after college. When the third book came out, it had taken off, and last year he had sold the movie rights for some obscene amount. Olivia didn't know all the details, but he and Quinn lived a very comfortable lifestyle off of the proceeds. After the book was first published, he'd bought his parents a house. It burned to the ground when he was visiting them, and his parents and brother lost their lives. Nicholas was badly injured when he jumped from a second story window.

"I think he carried a lot of survivor guilt over the fire that killed his family," Olivia said. "It sounded like he wasn't that close to his brother, but it really hit him hard losing his parents."

"It can be hard on people who survive a tragedy," Cruz said. "They find it hard to be grateful to be alive when people they love die suddenly or violently." A wave of sadness seemed to come over him, and Max remembered that his father, also a cop, had lost his life in the line of duty.

"Yes, and I don't know if he's gotten over it after all these years," Olivia said. "Four or five, I think."

"But he never wrote another book?" Detective Cruz asked. "Doesn't that seem odd to you?"

"I think losing his family was too traumatic." Olivia shook her head. "It's too bad, really. He writes beautifully. Have you read his books?"

"I'm more of a thriller guy," he admitted. "I understand they were dystopian. Isn't that what you call it?"

"Yes. But they were more than that." Olivia managed a smile. *"Immersion* is really an adventure story with wonderful characters. The main character has to make some difficult choices along the way. I don't want to give away too much in case you decide to read it someday."

Cruz looked at Olivia quizzically. "He doesn't seem that deep to me," he said.

Olivia laughed softly. "Quinn says the fire changed him, although she didn't know him before. He's more about living in the moment now. I didn't know him before the fire either. None of us did. Well, none of us except Gabby."

Olivia had more to say about her friend Quinn. She'd opened up a yoga studio after she married Nicholas. Ashley was a little wild in college, but then settled down and went to nursing school.

"I see," Detective Cruz said.

"Why are you asking so many questions about my friends?" Olivia asked. "They couldn't possibly have killed Gabby."

"The sooner he can eliminate you and your friends as suspects, the sooner he can focus on finding the person who killed Gabby," Max said to Olivia. She didn't want Olivia to know she thought one of her friends might be a murderer. "Right?" she said to Detective Cruz.

"Oh, yes. Right." He looked at his notepad, seemingly deep in thought. "Tell me more about Gabrielle."

Olivia filled him in about her childhood friend. "She came to visit me two years ago when I'd first moved here. It wasn't much of a visit to tell the truth. She kept disappearing, and I think she was doing drugs. I don't know how she managed to find drugs in Crystal Shores when she didn't know anyone here but me, but I guess addicts are good at that. She didn't seem out of it when she came back from wandering off. I haven't been around anyone who does drugs, so I don't know how to recognize the signs."

"Do you think she saw her dealer this trip?" he asked.

"She wasn't out of my sight from the time she arrived until she went down to the beach last night." Olivia thought for a moment, then added, "She did go into the other room to make some phone calls." She slowly shook her head. "No, she couldn't have met someone at the beach, could she? She didn't even know where the beach house was until we got there."

"But she could have called or texted someone from the beach house and arranged to meet them," Max said.

"I suppose so," Olivia admitted. "It just seems unlikely to me."

"You can check her phone," Max suggested to Detective Cruz.

"Her phone is missing," he said. "We got a search warrant for the beach house this morning, but it's nowhere to be found."

"Did you find anything else at the house?" Max hoped he was willing to share information.

He said no, but Max wondered if he were holding out. He stood to go, but looked like he had something else to say. Then, as if he'd thought better of it, he said, "I'll let you get back to your movie," and walked to the door. "Let me know if you remember anything else."

After the detective left, Quinn called from the beach house and invited Olivia to join them for take-out Chinese food. Max was also invited, and though she didn't feel much like socializing, solving the murder was her priority right now, so she accepted.

The sooner she could prove that Olivia and the others had nothing to do with Gabby's death, the sooner the police could focus on finding out who did.

CHAPTER TEN

Nicholas, Quinn, Ashley and Olivia dug into their garlic chicken and beef with broccoli. Max pretended to be engrossed in her food while watching them all out of the corner of her eye.

It gave her an uncomfortable feeling to even consider the idea that one of Olivia's friends might be a murderer. But then again, if she were going to clear them of suspicion, the best way to do it would be to think of them as suspects and remove them one by one from her list. She kept going back and forth in her mind from thinking one of them was a murderer to thinking it couldn't be any of them. She just had to keep an open mind and not come to any conclusions until the clues pointed her in the right direction.

Nicholas got up to open another bottle of wine. This group sure could put it away, but at least they weren't drinking double martinis tonight.

"I'm going to miss her, you know," Quinn said, putting her barely touched plate on the coffee table. "She was one of a kind to say the least."

"I thought you hadn't seen her in eight years," Max blurted out without thinking.

"I hadn't, but there's just something about knowing I'll never see her again. There are those people that when you see them it's just like you saw them a week ago. It was like that with Gabby. I just wish we could have talked so I could tell her there weren't any hard feelings."

"You mean about…" Olivia started to say, then her voice trailed off as Nicholas returned to the table and topped off their glasses. He sat back down next to Quinn and put his arm around her shoulders.

"Yes, about her and Nicholas. You can say it. It's ancient history as far as I'm concerned. I don't think Gabby came here to cause trouble."

"If you say so," Ashley said sarcastically. Max looked at the woman. Ashley hadn't liked Gabby and she didn't hide the fact. Max wondered why she seemed to carry such a grudge.

Max listened to everyone talk. Had any of them really known Gabby? Not the Gabby of childhood or college days, but the Gabby that had shown up in town a few days ago. Did people change? Max thought so, but plenty of people would disagree with her. Not even Olivia seemed to really know her long time friend.

After Quinn took everyone's plates into the kitchen, Ashley wandered out onto the veranda. She seemed like a loner, or perhaps she wasn't that close to her sister and her husband. Max followed her outside. This was her chance. The sky glowed orange from the last rays of the sun and a gentle breeze wafted across the veranda.

"How are you doing, Ashley? I mean, I know you didn't care for Gabby much, but it's still a shock."

Ashley had a faraway look in her eyes. "Life is short," she said. "And then you die."

"Well, that's one way to look at it," Max said, wondering how Ashley got to be so cynical at such a young age. Maybe she'd seen her share of illness and death as a nurse.

"How do you look at it?" Ashley asked, turning to face Max. There was a bitterness Max hadn't noticed before. She added softly, "She was my friend, too, you know."

"She was?" Max didn't try to hide her surprise.

"Olivia and Gabby were inseparable when Quinn first met them and then the three of them were always together. I showed up at Berkeley the next year and Gabby had pretty much given up on getting Olivia and Quinn to go out. They always wanted to study or get to bed early. Gabby and I would go to parties together and on Friday night, we'd get dressed up and go hit the clubs. We got into all the hottest places and never paid for a drink."

"So, what happened with you two?"

Ashley sighed and gazed out at the ocean. "She found someone else to party with. Started doing coke. Thought I was too straight laced. Me! Hah!"

"I'm sorry," Max said sincerely. "So now it's like you've lost her a second time."

Ashley abruptly turned back to Max. "Why all the questions? Do you think I killed her?"

Max was taken aback. "No," she stammered. "Of course not."

"Then why don't you leave me alone?" Ashley turned back to the sea, obviously done with their conversation.

Max stood unmoving for a moment, wanting to say something but not wanting to anger Ashley any more than she obviously had. She decided any other questions she had could wait until later and she went back inside.

Olivia's phone rang, and Max expected her to ignore it after she looked at the screen, since she had tired of people calling about the murder, but instead she jumped up from the sofa and answered it.

"Zach!" Olivia sounded happier than she had all day. She walked into the kitchen, and Max overheard her say, "I've been trying to call you." Olivia listened to him and then cried out, "That's wonderful! I'll be home right away. I just need to drop off Max." She ran back into the living room and announced, "Zach is home!"

Max protested that she could get a ride, but Olivia hushed her and ran around hugging everyone goodnight. Max and Olivia walked out the front door and once they were outside Olivia said, "I'm thrilled that Zach made it home early, but honestly, I'm glad for any reason to get out of there. I was trying to think of an excuse to leave when I got his phone call."

"You, too? I thought it was just me." Max felt more relaxed now that she was out of the house.

"You could cut the tension with a knife," Olivia said as they climbed into her car.

Max agreed. "Do you think it's because they all are under suspicion?"

"Maybe. I think they would have left town already if Detective Cruz hadn't told them to stay."

Max snickered. "He can't tell them to stay." She saw Olivia's look of curiosity. "Do you remember what he actually said? He said, 'I don't want you leaving town.' That's a whole different thing. It just sounds official. They're free to go unless he arrests them."

Olivia laughed. "That detective is a clever one."

They turned onto Max's street and pulled up in front of her dad's house. There wasn't a single light on that they could see.

"I guess my dad's out tonight," Max said.

"Do you want me to come up with you?" Olivia asked. "Or you can come stay with me again if you don't want to be alone."

"No, I'm fine." Max leaned over to give Olivia a hug then got out of the car. She walked around the side of the house to the back and up the stairs to her apartment. It seemed so quiet and she stood on the landing listening for the sound of crashing waves. On a quiet night if the wind was just right you could hear them faintly from her place.

She fixed herself a cup of chamomile tea, curled up on the sofa, and turned on the T.V. After flicking through all the channels, she realized she wasn't even paying attention to what was on the screen. She turned it off and got out her laptop. She searched the internet for Nicholas Buckley, but didn't learn anything new. Keiko was so much better at this. The funny thing was she found pictures all over the internet, but every one was the same photo, the one she had seen on the back of the book jacket. There were even stories asking "Where is he now?" Max wasn't able to find a single interview after the date of the fire.

As for Quinn Buckley, it was like she didn't exist, but maybe she used her maiden name, whatever that was. She assumed it would be the same as Ashley's, but she didn't know Ashley's last name. She'd have to ask Olivia and hope that she didn't question why she wanted the information.

Max set the laptop aside and looked at the clock. It wasn't even ten, too early to go to bed. She could read for a while, but she wasn't sure she could focus on a book right now. Then she remembered Nicholas's book. She had a key to her dad's house, so she went and found *Immersion* on his bookshelf. Two hours later, she couldn't keep her eyes open, but she didn't want to stop reading, having been totally sucked into the story. The main character Alfred was journeying to a rumored land called Elysian where there was food and shelter for everyone, not just the wealthy. Just when he escaped one close call he faced another danger, from the people he ran into to trying to navigate the rough terrain. She finally gave in to her drooping eyelids and went to bed.

CHAPTER ELEVEN

Max's phone alarm awoke her at six thirty. She groaned. She really wasn't a morning person, but she had a reason for not sleeping in this morning. She especially hoped to run into Detective Cruz on the beach today, so she turned the alarm off and got dressed. If the detective went on a morning jog, he was always there at seven sharp. She thought punctuality was a good trait, as long as you didn't carry it too far.

Max pulled on her yoga pants and got a tee shirt out of her drawer, noticing the wrinkles in it. Oh well, the only way she would ever be free from wrinkles was if she bought an iron, and that wasn't going to happen. Besides, who ironed tee shirts? Lori probably did. Or maybe she sent them to the cleaners.

Why was she being so catty about a woman she'd only met once? She knew the answer to that question. It was because Lori had stolen Jason's heart. She grabbed a sweatshirt, locked her front door and headed down the stairs.

Detective Cruz was probably too perfect for her anyway. There never was a wrinkle in any of his clothes. It bothered her more than she liked to admit that he'd found a girlfriend. He was handsome, that was for sure, but he also seemed kind and in rare moments he displayed a sense of humor that she learned was more evident when he wasn't on duty.

She came out of her daydream and looked up and down the beach. The wind chilled her and she zipped up her sweatshirt, shoving her hands in her pockets. A thick mist hung over the water. No Detective Jason Cruz to be seen anywhere. Maybe he thought she was still mad at him and was avoiding her. Maybe she *was* still mad. She hadn't quite decided.

"Everything isn't about you," she told herself out loud. After all, he needed to solve a murder. Maybe he didn't have time for a morning jog. Or maybe he was sleeping in. Or maybe he was somewhere warm with a nice cup of coffee. Max shivered. That sounded wonderful right now. Maybe he was with Lori, she thought, scowling at the thought.

She resisted the urge to turn around and go home. The waves crashed violently against the shore, a sure sign that there was a tropical storm off the coast of Baja. June was early in the year for a storm, but it wasn't unheard of. Max knew the crashing waves would deposit sea glass on the beach, so she strolled along the edge of the shore, searching for flashes of color. Listening to the waves and the seagulls crying out she forgot about the murder, the wedding, and even Detective Cruz. She wandered along the edge of the water and barely noticed the boulders as she passed them. An eerie feeling came over her as she realized she had reached the little cove where Gabby had been killed. In her mind, she saw Gabby's body lying lifeless on the sand. She felt her skin prickle and looked around, feeling as if she was being watched.

Standing completely still, she listened for a sound, but only heard the sound of the crashing waves. She turned around slowly, stepping back just in time to avoid a wave. She saw something among the pebbles—a flash of green and silver. As the wave receded, she came closer and saw a ring. Gabby's ring. It had to be hers. She snatched it before the next wave could carry it away and ran back to the dry sand.

Turning it over in her hands she saw it was an exquisite emerald ring, Art Deco in style with intricate details. She dialed Jason's number, which she had programmed into her phone last summer.

"I've got Gabby's ring," she said when he picked up. "I found it on the beach. Someone must have thrown it into the water and it washed back up."

"You didn't touch it, did you?" he asked.

"Yes, I touched it. It would have been washed away if I hadn't. Besides, there couldn't possibly be any fingerprints on it after being in the water, could there?"

Max could almost hear him sigh over the phone. "Well, we'll never know now, will we?"

"No need to get snippy about it," Max said, not trying to hide her annoyance. She'd just found an important clue. "If the killer threw it into the ocean, then that means that theft wasn't the motive." Besides, anyone who would throw away a valuable ring must not need money. What suspects were left other than Olivia's friends?

"I'll worry about the motive, Max," he said. "Stay there and I'll send Officer Daniels over to get it from you. You can show him where you found it."

He hung up before Max could chastise him for being condescending. He didn't sound the least bit grateful that she'd found the ring. Maybe that was too much to expect.

If Gabby hadn't been killed for the ring, then what other motive would a stranger have? None. The ring must have been taken off Gabby's finger and tossed in the ocean to make it look like a robbery. Max felt convinced at that moment the murderer had to be someone Gabby knew. Did that mean it was Nicholas, Quinn, or Ashley? There was also the possibility that she'd met with a drug dealer who might have been the person that Nicholas had seen. Was Gabby's phone also in the ocean? Without the phone, Max didn't know how they would find out who the mysterious, shaggy-haired man was. Would Detective Cruz be able to find out what calls and texts Gabby had made from her cell phone provider? If he did, he probably wouldn't share that information with Max anyway.

After Officer Daniels left with the ring, she walked home at a brisk pace. In spite of the murder, she still had a shop to run and she would be late if she didn't hurry. Figuring out who killed Gabby would just have to wait.

CHAPTER TWELVE

Mondays were catch up days for Max at Wedding Belles Bridal Salon. After a hectic Saturday, it gave her a chance to place orders and make plans for the week plus catch up on sewing and alterations. She didn't make appointments on Mondays with rare exceptions.

Keiko had the day off, since Max didn't think they both needed to work six days a week. Besides, Keiko didn't want to work too many hours since she attended design school and had her own business designing and maintaining websites. Max wished she were available full time, since she could really use the help. They'd talked about hiring another assistant, but so far, that's all it had been. Talk.

All in all, Max enjoyed her quiet Mondays, but when she arrived at the shop and saw two women waiting at the door, she threw all ideas of a relaxing day out the window. One was a tall, curvy blonde and the other was shorter, with dark, curly hair and big, almond-shaped brown eyes.

"Good morning." Max hoped her voice sounded cheerful and welcoming. She really didn't like surprises and drop-in clients always stressed her out. "Have you come to look at wedding gowns?" She unlocked the front door and led them into the showroom.

They both started speaking at once. It turned out that they were friends who had ordered their wedding gowns from Antoine's Bridal.

"We just found out we won't be able to get our dresses. We need to order new ones, and fast," one of the women said.

"Our sample sale is in September," Max said. "Perhaps you can find something then?"

One of the brides was getting married in September and the other in August. "That's why I'm in such a panic," one of them said and the other agreed. "Everyone says it will take at least four months even on a rush order."

"And we haven't found anyone who's having a sample sale until at least September," the other woman said. "We read your online reviews and you sound like a miracle worker. We really need a miracle right now. We heard you make custom gowns. How long would that take?"

Max made it a rule never to rush custom gowns. "You would need to allow at least six months or longer depending on the design."

"It probably wouldn't be in our budget anyway," the brunette said, her shoulders slumping in defeat. "We put big deposits down on our gowns and we have no idea if we're going to get any of our money back."

"That's terrible." Max thought for a moment, but didn't know how she could help the women. She felt awful that a bridal shop would just close down and leave their customers without any alternatives. How could they do such a thing? "Why don't you give me your phone numbers and email addresses. If I come up with any ideas, I'll let you know."

The two women brightened and Max worried about giving them false hope. After they wrote down their information and left, she stood in the middle of the showroom thinking about what she could do for them. The one woman looked to be a size eight and the other a twelve, so they could get dresses off the rack and have them altered. She went to the office to research and see if any shops in Southern California had sample sales coming up. When she came up empty, she expanded her search to Northern California and Las Vegas. Still no luck.

She heard the front door jingle and found Fiona in the showroom. Fiona and her sister Teresa owned Knitpickers, the yarn store next door. Neither sister looked their ages, which was somewhere in the seventies. She wore an oversized tee shirt that said "Forget Me Knot" with leggings and a black bedazzled baseball cap.

"How are you, my dear?" Fiona asked and gave Max a hug.

"I'm doing all right," Max said. The truth was she wasn't sure how she was feeling. In some ways, everything seemed completely normal, but nothing was normal about murder.

"I'm all on edge, what with a murderer being on the loose. It's simply shocking!"

"Yes, I—"

"And poor Olivia. How is she holding up? She must be devastated. Is she going through with the wedding? I hope she does."

"As far as I know," Max said, finally able to get a word in. "She's been planning it for six months. You can't just reschedule a wedding on such short notice."

"I feel so bad for her," Fiona said. "She's such a sweet girl. Did you know her friend? I heard she was from out of town."

"Yes, she just arrived on Saturday. It's so sad. She was only thirty years old."

The door jingled again and Teresa entered wearing a flowing sky blue tunic. Her long, silver hair fell down her back in a single braid. "You forgot Max's present," she said to her sister.

Max took the gift bag from Teresa and pulled out a crocheted purse. At least she thought that's what it was. "It's the exact color of my bridesmaid dress!"

Fiona grinned. "I dyed it myself. I got a scrap of the fabric from Keiko so I could match the color."

"Look inside," Teresa said, impatiently. "It's your maid of honor emergency kit. There are tissues, breath mints, blotting papers, oh, and a tiny pair of scissors in a little case. Basically, everything I could think of that Olivia might need."

"It's perfect." The bag was full of things that might be useful on Olivia's wedding day. Max hadn't even thought of having an emergency kit. She hugged Teresa. "Thank you, both of you. It's lovely and it will definitely come in handy."

"So, any news on who the murderer might be?" Fiona asked. Max had a feeling that the real reason Fiona had stopped by was to get some gossip.

"None," Max said. She didn't want to divulge any details. The sisters, Fiona especially, were not known for keeping information to themselves. She didn't want the killer to find out that the ring had been found, at least not until the police decided to release that information.

Teresa shook her head sadly. "The poor girl was so young. I just don't understand the world today."

"There have always been murderers," Fiona said. "Ever since Cain and Abel."

"I suppose you're right," Teresa admitted. "I'd better get back to the shop and check on Josie. It's not a good idea to leave a cat alone with a store full of yarn for too long."

"Is Simon still dropping her off at your shop every morning?" Max asked.

Teresa smiled dreamily. "Yes, every day but Sunday, since we're closed."

Teresa had met Simon Abbott when she found his cat Josie over a year ago. Since then, the two seniors had been dating. Simon dropped Josie off every day at the knitting shop and picked her up at the end of the day. Max was thrilled that Teresa had a second shot at love.

"Let us know if you learn anything about the murder," Fiona whispered to Max. Then, to her sister she said, "Let's go check on that darn cat."

There were no surprises for the rest of the morning, and at noon Max closed the shop to go to her favorite deli for a pastrami sandwich. When she got back, she was surprised to see Quinn standing by the front door. Max unlocked the door and offered Quinn a cup of tea.

"No, thank you. I was just out running errands, and when I saw your shop I thought I'd stop by for a few moments. I hope you don't mind me dropping in on you. I'm worried about Olivia. She seems to be taking it harder than anyone."

"Olivia grew up with Gabby. Of course, she's upset. It will take her a while to recover from the shock of what she saw, but now that Zach's back, I think she'll be fine. Or at least better." Max wondered if that was the only reason for the visit.

"I'm sure you're right," Olivia said.

"Water?" Max asked.

"Thank you, that would be great."

Max got two waters out of the office fridge and handed one to Quinn. As Quinn opened it, she asked, "Do you think they'll go through with the wedding?"

"Oh, I don't know," Max said. "I don't think she's had a chance to talk it over with Zach. I really hope they do."

"We'd just like to get home if there's not going to be a wedding," Quinn said. "It hasn't turned out to be much of a vacation. It's the first time I've talked Nicholas into going out of town for more than a year."

Max hid her surprise at Quinn's lack of sensitivity. It seemed selfish of her to think of her vacation at a time like this. "I think Olivia could really use the moral support from her friends right now." She didn't want the three friends to leave before the murder was solved, but they could leave any time they chose. That made it especially important to get to the truth fast.

Quinn looked up at Max with wide eyes. "Oh, of course. I didn't mean... I just thought now that Zach's back, she'd rather be with him. But maybe I'll see if Ashley and I can take them out to dinner tonight. We at least want a chance to meet Zach while we're here."

"I think she'd like that." Quinn was one of Olivia's closest friends, but Max began to have second thoughts about sending

Olivia out to dinner with two murder suspects. She'd have to text Olivia so she could be ready with an excuse if she wanted to beg off.

"The police were back to question us yesterday," Quinn said. "Did that detective talk to you again, too?"

"Yes, Detective Cruz stopped by Olivia's when I was there and questioned both of us again."

"Has he figured out who the person was that Nicholas and Ashley saw?" Quinn asked.

"I don't think so, but he's a very good detective. I'm sure he'll find out who murdered your friend."

"Well, good," Quinn said and stood to go. "I'm sorry we're not getting to know each other under better circumstances."

"At least we finally got to meet. Olivia's talked about you so many times, I almost felt like I knew you before I met you. I hope you'll be able to come and visit again soon." That was, of course, assuming none of them was a murderer.

"We'll see. Nicholas doesn't like to travel much these days. He's practically a recluse. I have to force him just to go out to a restaurant for dinner. It took me weeks to talk him into coming for the wedding."

Max was surprised that Quinn's husband would have been so reluctant to make a short trip to see her friend get married. "Well then, just come by yourself," Max said. "He can spare you for a few days, can't he?"

Quinn gave Max a look that told her how impossible that idea was. But why couldn't a wife travel without her husband? Nicholas didn't seem so helpless that he couldn't be left home alone.

"We'll see," Quinn repeated, but Max knew by the way she said it that the answer was no. "I'd better get back to the house." She walked toward the door and then paused and turned around smiling. "I'm really glad Olivia has found such a good friend. I'll see you tomorrow."

"Tomorrow?"

"Yes," Quinn said. "Ashley and I are bringing our dresses to be hemmed. Remember?"

"Oh, yes," Max said. She had completely forgotten, but wasn't about to admit it. "See you then."

Quinn seemed almost wistful that her friendship with Olivia wasn't what it used to be. Had Nicholas become like an albatross forcing her to keep her husband company in his self-imposed exile? Max knew she could never live that way, but reminded herself that love made you do strange things.

oOo

Shortly after Quinn left, Darlene Chandler came in through the back door. Max greeted her old boss warmly, but wondered if she were there to check up on her. When Darlene had sold her the shop, she'd kept a minority interest and stayed on in a consulting role. They were supposed to meet once a week, but lately her mentor had been dropping by more often, and Max didn't know why.

Darlene's dark hair was pulled back in a bun, her signature style, and she wore a conservative pantsuit with sensible shoes. In fact, if there were one word to describe Darlene and how she lived her life, it would be "sensible."

"I'll never get used to these hardwood floors. They just wouldn't have been acceptable in my day," Darlene said, her low heels making a clicking sound against the wood.

Max was used to Darlene's comments about what was or was not acceptable "in her day." It used to bug her when she was the employee and had to do as she was told, but now she was the boss and could shrug off Darlene's comments. In spite of her old fashioned ideas, Darlene had been indispensable with her advice about running the shop. There was so much more involved in being a business owner than Max had realized. "What brings you around today?" Max asked. "I thought we were meeting for lunch on Friday."

"I heard about the murder," Darlene said. "It was someone you knew, wasn't it?"

"I'd just met her that day. She was one of Olivia's friends." Max wasn't surprised by her mentor's curiosity. It seemed as though everyone in town wanted to know details about the murder. Max didn't volunteer information, but answered Darlene's questions briefly, not telling her anything that hadn't been in the papers.

"Any idea who killed her?" Darlene asked. "I'd sleep better if I knew whoever did it was locked up."

"Well, the police haven't arrested anyone yet," Max said.

"That's disappointing," Darlene said, and looked around the room, her eyes coming to rest on the rack of gowns that lined the wall. "Did the new shipment of dresses arrive?"

"Yes, they were delivered Friday," Max said. "I'm about halfway through steaming them. Would you like to take a look?"

The two women walked upstairs where overflow inventory was kept. Max showed her a freshly steamed gown that she hadn't yet covered in plastic. It was an off-the-shoulder chiffon gown with a flounce around the top, giving it the feel of a peasant dress. A very fancy peasant dress.

Darlene scowled at the dress. "I fought you on ordering those off-the-shoulder gowns, but I was at Fashion Island today and half the women seemed to be wearing off the shoulder blouses and dresses."

"Well, I only ordered a few, really," Max said. "It was a small risk. That's what you taught me. Take small risks. Not big ones."

Darlene smiled at Max acknowledging her words of wisdom. "I'm glad you took my advice," she said.

Darlene's advice was not to order any of the dresses, but Max wasn't about to remind her of that.

"Are you sure you can't use me for more hours?" Darlene asked. "I have some free time I can spare you. With Keiko working part time, you must be extremely busy."

Max needed another assistant, not an ex-boss. She wouldn't feel comfortable telling Darlene to sweep the floors or steam gowns. Darlene was used to being the one to order people around.

"Is retirement not agreeing with you? I thought you and Kenneth were going to see the country, but you haven't done any traveling in months."

"We spent one month in a Winnebago and saw as much of the country as I care to see. No matter how much you love someone, a month in cramped quarters will test your relationship."

"Maybe you need a hobby," Max suggested.

"I garden, but that only takes a few hours a week," Darlene said. "I don't have any other hobbies. My work always took up most of my time. I can help with the bookkeeping," she suggested.

"Keiko takes care of that and she sends everything to the accountant."

"Fine." Darlene sounded disappointed. "I guess I'll leave you to get back to work."

The door jingled and River, their mailman, entered. "Morning, Max," the middle-aged surfer said. As usual, his thinning, sandy blond hair was pulled back in a ponytail. "Nice to see you Darlene," he added. "How are you enjoying retirement?"

"I'm not," she huffed.

"Sorry to hear that," he said. "You know what Lao-Tse says."

"I don't care what Lao-Tse says," Darlene grumbled. "I'm bored." She turned and headed for the back door.

"See you Friday," Max called out after her, hoping Darlene would be in better spirits by then. Turning back to River, she said, "I'm sure she didn't mean to be rude. She doesn't seem very happy these days. I wonder if she regrets selling her business and retiring. She has a lot of life left in her and I don't think she's ready to ride into the sunset."

"She has to live with her choices. As Eleanor Roosevelt said--" He stopped mid-sentence. "Would you like to know what Eleanor Roosevelt said?"

"Are you kidding?" Max grinned. "Of course, I do!" Max loved the seemingly endless supply of inspirational quotes River dispensed regularly.

River beamed back at her. "She said, 'The choices we make are ultimately our responsibility.' I know you want to help everyone, Max, but she's made her choice and she needs to find her own way."

"I suppose you're right River. I just don't like to see anyone unhappy. I suppose she'll figure it out on her own. Thanks."

"I suppose you're investigating the murder of that poor girl," he said softly.

"I'm just telling them what I know," Max said, not wanting to tell River she was working hard to find out who had killed Gabby.

River looked at her with skepticism. "Just promise me you'll be careful."

"Of course," she said with a smile.

"Namaste," he said, and walked out the door on his way to finish his route and share his wisdom around the neighborhood.

CHAPTER THIRTEEN

Max had planned to work on alterations today, and hoped there wouldn't be any more interruptions. She needed her quiet Mondays to catch up on all her work. She thought again about hiring another assistant. Maybe she'd bring it up with Keiko tomorrow and see what she thought of the idea. She was in the middle of taking out stitches with her seam ripper when the door jingled. Emerging from the workroom, she froze as soon as she saw who had entered. Lori stood there looking even more perfect than she did when Max first met her. She wore a sleek black pantsuit and four-inch heeled pumps. Her blond hair fell past her shoulders in soft curls. Max wondered how long it took her to look so effortlessly pulled together.

"Hello," Max said, thinking there were only two reasons Detective Cruz's girlfriend would be in her shop and not liking either one. Her stomach tied itself in a knot. Lori either wanted to talk or she wanted a wedding dress. She hoped it was the former, although what she would want to talk to Max about she couldn't imagine.

"Hi, Max," Lori said cheerfully. "What a lovely shop you have. I was driving by and saw your sign and thought I'd stop in and say hello."

"Hello," Max repeated, not knowing what else to say. They stood there in awkward silence for a moment.

Finally, Lori spoke. "Do you have time to talk?"

So she wanted to talk. Max felt a wave of relief. Hopefully she didn't want to talk about a wedding dress. She looked at Lori's hand, but didn't see an engagement ring. "Sure, what can I do for you?"

"You must be wondering what I'm doing here."

No kidding. "Well, yes," Max said, doing her best to regain her composure and going into autopilot hostess mode. "Would you like some tea? I just made a pot."

"I don't really care for tea," Lori said. "Do you have any coffee?"

"Sure." Max motioned for her to sit down and went in her office. A coffee machine in the office made single cups, so she put in a pod and waited for the cup to fill. What would Jason's girlfriend want to talk to her about? The only thing they had in common was Jason. Did she want to talk about him? That was a conversation she didn't want to have. The coffee finished pouring and she couldn't put off the conversation any longer. She put the cup in front of Lori and sat down across from her with her tea. "Sugar?" she asked, holding out the bowl of sugar cubes.

"No, thank you," Lori said, and took a sip of her black coffee. "Mmm, it's delicious."

Max added one sugar to her tea and stirred it longer than necessary, waiting for Lori to tell her why she was there. Ms. Perfect finally got to the point.

"Jason hasn't officially proposed yet, but when he does, I don't expect it to be a long engagement. How long does it take to order a wedding dress?"

Max felt her mouth go dry and took a sip of tea to buy her some time before replying. Was Jason really going to marry this woman? Max hadn't dated anyone for a year because no one else made her pulse race the way Jason did. And now he was going to propose to someone else. She suddenly hated this woman that she didn't even know. She realized Lori was expecting an answer. What was the question?

Max swallowed and tried to sound nonchalant. "I'm sorry, what?"

Lori smiled sweetly. "How long should I allow to order a wedding dress?"

"Oh. Well, it's good to allow at least six months, but eight is better. Four or five months for the dress to arrive and then time for alterations. Alterations shouldn't be extensive unless you've gained or lost a lot of weight. A lot of women try to lose weight for the wedding, but you don't... I mean, you look fine the way you are." Max realized she was rambling and stopped speaking abruptly. Luckily, Lori didn't seem to be aware of her distress.

"I'd love to try on some dresses," Lori said. "I wouldn't get a wedding dress from anyone but you. Partly because you and Jason are friends, but also because you have an amazing reputation. I looked you up online."

Max wasn't sure how she would survive the whole ordeal of helping Lori pick a wedding gown. She certainly wasn't going to do it alone. She needed Keiko for moral support.

"I'd be happy to make an appointment for you," Max said, and retrieved her laptop from the office. Sitting back down she asked, "How's next week sound?" Or next year. Or never.

"Oh, don't you have something sooner? Maybe Wednesday? My mom's in town and I'd love her to be there."

Max stared at the computer screen. There wasn't a single appointment booked for Wednesday. Not used to coming up with excuses on short notice, she said, "Morning or afternoon?"

"How's four?" Lori asked.

"Okay," Max heard herself say. "Four o'clock it is."

"And if you see Jason, would you not mention to him that we met? I want to be the one to tell him."

"Sure," Max agreed. She didn't want to have that conversation with Detective Cruz anyway.

Lori stood up to go and for a horrified moment, Max thought she was going to give her a hug. Instead, she turned and walked to the door.

"See you Wednesday," Lori said as she opened the door.

"See you." Can't wait.

After Lori left, Max stared at the computer screen and the appointment seemed to taunt her. She really wanted to cry, but told herself not to be childish. After all, she hardly knew Jason. Sure he was intelligent, compassionate, and thoughtful. And he was handsome. But he could be inflexible at times and he was very fastidious. He wasn't perfect. There were plenty of other men in the world, and one must be right for her. But she didn't want any of them. She wanted Jason. For the first time, she admitted it to herself, and now it was too late.

Max didn't want to bother Olivia with her silly problems, but on the other hand, maybe the distraction would be a good thing, so she called her friend.

"No!" Olivia said, sounding shocked. "She didn't!"

"She sure did," Max said.

"She's shopping for a wedding dress and he hasn't even proposed? That is the height of presumption."

"Well," Max said, "they must have talked about it. Didn't you and Zach talk about marriage before he proposed?"

"Yes, but that's not the point," Olivia said. "I didn't ask you to make my gown until I had a ring on my finger."

Max sighed. "What's wrong with me? First Andy, and now this. I keep falling for guys who aren't interested in me."

"Nothing is wrong with you," Olivia assured her. "He is interested in you. I'm sure of it. I've seen the way he looks at you."

Max felt a glimmer of hope, which she quickly dismissed. Max had felt there was something between them, but obviously she'd been mistaken. "Olivia. He has a girlfriend. A serious girlfriend. A girlfriend he's talking about marriage with."

"Yes. He has a girlfriend. I'll admit, that's somewhat of an impediment. But she's a girlfriend. Not a fiancée. I don't believe for a minute that he's going to marry her. I didn't even expect him to invite her to the wedding or I would have warned you." Olivia sounded perturbed. "Isn't there some way for you to get out of helping her with her wedding gown? That's gonna suck."

"Big time," Max agreed. "I could pretend to be sick that day and let Keiko help her."

"You could, but you're not going to, right?"

"No," Max admitted. "She'd probably just reschedule. I might as well get it over with."

"I wish I could take you out tonight, but I'm going out with Quinn and Ashley," Olivia said.

"You are?" Apparently Olivia wasn't as suspicious as she was. "Be careful, okay?"

Olivia laughed. "Don't tell me you think they're suspects."

"Okay, I won't tell you." Max didn't want to tell her friend her suspicions.

Olivia gasped. "You really do consider them suspects."

"It's just that I don't think it was a stranger. It must have been someone she knew. Someone with a motive."

"So you think it was one of my friends?" Olivia sounded incredulous." Really? Don't be ridiculous."

"Okay," Max said, bristling a little at being called ridiculous. "I won't be ridiculous if you won't be too trusting."

"It's a deal," Olivia said.

"And don't call me ridiculous when I'm just watching out for you."

"Sorry," Olivia said. "Thank you for caring and being there for me. You just don't know my friends as well as I do."

"But you don't know Nicholas that well, do you?" She knew Olivia hadn't spent much time with Quinn's husband.

"No, but Quinn does. And I trust Quinn. Quinn is one of the most honest people I know. In college, one of our classmates got the answers to one of our final exams and Quinn refused to look at it. And she quit being friends with that person because she was a cheater. If she married Nicholas, then I'm sure he's a good guy, even if he is a bit sullen and withdrawn at times."

Max wished she trusted the three friends the way Olivia did. She should trust Olivia's judgment, but she had to keep an open mind if she were going to solve a murder.

"Was it possible that there was someone else in town who knew Gabby?" Max asked.

Olivia was silent for a moment. "I don't think so, but then, when she was here two summers ago she kept disappearing for an hour or two at a time. She'd say she was going for a walk. I'd offer to go along, but she'd say she just wanted some alone time."

She felt bad about practically accusing Olivia's friends of murder. She had called Olivia to get her mind off Gabby's death, and actually ended up upsetting her more. But she'd learned something. If Gabby spent that much time away from Olivia when she'd visited, maybe she went to meet someone. She needed to find out who that someone might be.

"Hello," Olivia said. "You still there?"

"Sorry. Do you have any idea if she was meeting someone when she went for her walks?"

"No idea. If she knew anyone else in town, it's news to me. I'd better get back to work. And as for Lori, I wouldn't worry about her too much. I think this wedding thing is all in her mind."

"What makes you say that?"

"I've seen the way he looks at her." Olivia said. "And I've seen the way he looks at you."

Max felt her face redden. "But he's going out with her, not me."

"Just give it a little time. You'll see."

It was remarkable how much better Max felt about Lori after talking with Olivia. She'd probably feel even better after talking with Eric. After calling him, he showed up at her shop minutes later. His shop, Flower to the People, was just a few doors down.

Eric was tall and handsome, with dark hair and eyelashes to die for. All her classmates had been jealous of her when she brought a mature, sophisticated date to prom. They didn't need to know Eric was doing her mom a favor taking her to the dance. They also didn't need to know he was gay. They stayed up half the night talking at a coffee shop after prom and were fast friends ever since.

Eric arrived with an enormous tropical bouquet that complemented the color scheme of the shop. He placed it on the coffee table in the center of the showroom.

"That's what the shop has been missing," Max said. The floral display was the perfect focal point and added a touch of elegance to the shop. "How much would you charge me to bring me a bouquet like this every week?"

"It should last two weeks," Eric said. "You may need to remove a few flowers that might wilt sooner than that, but it will still look just as stunning. And I won't charge you if you put a few brochures on the table next to it."

"Are you kidding?" Max grinned. "That's wonderful!"

"Now, what are we going to do about Detective Cruz's new girlfriend?" Eric voiced his indignation and said Jason was a fool and Lori, who he'd never met, was a bimbo, which made Max laugh.

He plopped down on the sofa and she offered him something to drink, which he turned down. "Who shops for a dress when they haven't even been proposed to?" he huffed. "That reeks of desperation."

"Lori seems like someone who is used to getting what she wants," Max said, perching on the edge of an easy chair.

"Besides, they must have talked about marriage, or she wouldn't be so sure he was going to propose."

"You should have asked him out when I told you to," Eric said. "I did tell you to, didn't I?"

"No, actually, you didn't." She hadn't seen much of the detective in the past year until a few weeks ago when she'd learned he liked to go on early morning jogs on the beach. She had considered asking him out for coffee or something. She just didn't expect him to have a girlfriend once she got up the nerve.

"I meant to. I suppose it's too late now. Unless we can figure out a way to break them up. Maybe Keiko could find something unsavory in her past. She's so good with all that computer stuff." He looked at Max who merely raised her eyebrows at this suggestion. "Are you going to be okay?"

"Of course," Max said, laughing. She didn't want her friends to know just how disappointed she really was. "I hardly know Jason. He might have some really annoying habits that would have driven me crazy. Have you ever noticed that he never has a hair out of place or a wrinkle in his clothes?"

"What in the world is wrong with that?" Eric asked.

Max looked at Eric, who was always impeccably dressed and perfectly groomed. "Nothing," she murmured.

"How's Olivia holding up?" he asked. "I mean with the murder and everything."

"Oh, yes, the murder. I'm so selfish thinking about myself when she's just lost a friend. She's holding up about as well as can be expected," she said. "She's thinking about cancelling the wedding."

"No!" Eric exclaimed. "She can't! I have been looking forward to this wedding for months. I've designed a bridal bouquet to die for. Just wait till you see it. If you even get to see it." He sounded forlorn.

"Well," Max said, "it's not all about you, you know."

"It's always about me," he said. "Don't you realize that by now?"

Max laughed. "You're right. I don't know what I was thinking. I'll tell Olivia she can't cancel because you'll be disappointed."

"Good. I'm glad that's settled. Now, I've got to get back to the shop before Daphne does any damage."

"You've really got to get a new assistant, Eric. One that can run the shop for ten minutes without you."

"What, and fire Daphne?" He sounded outraged at the idea. "I could never do that. If I really wanted to get rid of her, I'd just be mean to her until she quit. But I can't be mean to her. She's so adorable. Besides, she makes me laugh."

Max just shook her head. "Well, I understand not wanting to fire someone. I've got Keiko to make me laugh but she's also indispensable. I don't know what I would do if I ever had to fire someone."

"You could always have Darlene do it for you. She was very good at firing people."

Max laughed. "She really was. We used to go through assistants like…" She tried to think of the right word.

"Like I go through hair gel," Eric said. "I buy it by the case."

"Well, say hi to Daphne for me."

Eric gave Max a hug and assured her that she was too good for Detective Cruz and there was someone out there who would be perfect for her.

After Eric left, Max felt adrift. She got started on alterations on a wedding gown for one of their clients, but after the third time she had to rip out stitches, she realized she was not in the right state of mind for sewing. There was nothing else that really needed to be done for the day, and she didn't want to sit around feeling sorry for herself. She'd never closed early since she'd taken over ownership of the shop, but she was the boss now and she could do what she wanted. Besides, it was five o'clock, so it wasn't that early. She swept and vacuumed then locked the front door and walked the four blocks to her home.

CHAPTER FOURTEEN

Max worried about Olivia going out with Quinn and Ashley. She hoped she'd taken her warning seriously, but Olivia was such a trusting soul, she'd probably never suspect one of her friends of doing something so terrible.

After the short walk home, Max decided to stop in to see her dad. If he happened to have leftovers, that was just a bonus.

She walked through his front door without knocking as usual. She frowned. He was always telling her to be careful, but he'd left his front door unlocked. She'd have to talk to him about that.

"Dad?" She called out, but didn't get an answer. She found him in the courtyard that separated his house from the garage and her apartment above it. He was watering the plants she had been ignoring. The wilted hydrangeas seemed to perk up with the attention. Sparrows chirped loudly in the shrubs that stood against the fence.

"Hi, sunshine," he said when he saw her step out the back door. "How was your day?"

"Fine," she said. "A bit surreal in a way. Brides kept dropping in wanting wedding gowns in a rush. I don't know if I'll be able to help them."

"Why are they dropping in all of a sudden?"

"Antoine's Bridal has declared bankruptcy and isn't delivering wedding gowns that have been ordered."

"They can't expect you to work miracles," he said.

"Well, apparently they do. I just feel so bad for them. I'd like to help if I can."

"Would you turn the water off?" he asked. "I'm sure you'll think of something. You're resourceful. And you love helping people."

"I really do," Max admitted. It was the favorite part of her job.

She didn't mention the murder or her suspicions. Her tendency to get involved in murder investigations did not sit well with him. She knew he wanted his daughter to be safe, and she didn't want him to worry, so sometimes the less he knew the better. And she certainly wasn't going to tell him about Lori stopping by. She'd never confided in him about her feelings for Jason.

"I was about to make myself a grilled cheese," he said, winding the hose up and hanging it back on the wall. "Want one?"

"Thanks, Dad. I'd love one." He made the best buttery grilled cheese sandwiches. "Why don't we eat out here? It's turning into a lovely evening."

She and her father had become closer after her mother passed away, and she didn't know what she'd do without him. Go hungry a lot of the time, for starters.

"So you decided to take a break from painting and do some gardening?" she asked, following him back inside.

"I took a break from doing the books. I never realized how much work the business side of painting involved. Your mother took care of all of that for me. I'm just not a numbers person."

115

He got the bread and cheese out of the refrigerator and started making their sandwiches. Max poured them both a glass of lemonade, then sat down and watched him fry up their dinner.

"I'm lucky I have Keiko to help with the books, plus an accountant to handle all the taxes."

"I have an accountant, but she doesn't take care of the day to day things," Richard said. "Plus, I've been trying to learn about marketing. There's so much information online it's overwhelming. At least I have the website Keiko made for me. I get emails almost every day from it. I got an email from someone in Florida who's thinking of buying one of my paintings. Isn't that crazy?"

"Not these days. Have you thought about taking a class? There must be one about running a small business."

"I took a basic accounting class at the senior center, but it wasn't really tailored to someone like me."

"But you're not a senior," Max said.

Richard laughed. "I guess I'm old enough for them. You can join if you're 55."

"Well, there must be a lot of seniors who start their own businesses after they retire. You'd think the senior center would have a class tailored to them." A thought popped into her head. Maybe there was a way to solve two problems with one stone. "Hey, I have an idea. You should call Darlene. I bet she'd be happy to help you with learning more about business and marketing."

"You think she has the time?"

"I know she has the time. She's bored to death with retirement and I bet she'd jump at the chance to help you."

"Great! I'll give her a call later."

They took their sandwiches and lemonades back out to the courtyard. Max's mind drifted to the murder. Nicholas would be at the beach house alone. Perhaps without the others around she'd be able to ask him what he had been arguing with Gabby about that night. "Can I borrow your car this evening?" she asked.

"Sure," he said. "Going to see Olivia?"

"I'm going to stop by the beach house and see how everyone's doing. I don't think Olivia's been in the mood to be much of a hostess." She felt a little guilty not telling him she was really going to talk to Nicholas, but she didn't want him to try to change her mind.

"That's understandable. Losing someone you care about is never easy." He cleared his throat. It would be a long time before he got over losing Max's mom. "The rumor around town is that someone surprised Gabby on the beach and robbed her. She must have fought back, so they killed her."

"That's a possibility." She wished that was the case, but she knew Gabby hadn't fought back and it appeared less and less likely that the killer had been a stranger. A stranger had no motive that she could see. It was bad enough that one of Olivia's friends was dead. What if another was a murderer?

"I hope the police find out who did it. I don't like the idea that there might be a killer on the loose. I hope you're being safe. You lock the door as soon as you come home, right?"

"Yes, I do. And you need to do the same."

"You're right," he agreed. "I've always felt so safe in our little town, but I should be more careful. I was thinking of putting a security screen door on your place."

"Ugh. They're so ugly." Max didn't like that idea at all. "How about a security camera instead?"

"Someone could still break in. You'd just see who it was." He sounded like his mind was made up. "With a security door you could leave your front door open to let the breeze in."

Max decided to change the subject. "I borrowed Nicholas's book last night. It was so good I didn't want to put it down."

"It's been years since I read it, but I remember loving it. Have you gotten to the point where the main character finds his brother?"

"Alfred has a brother?"

"Oops," Richard said. "I hope I didn't spoil it."

"Just don't say anything else about it," Max said. "I'll probably finish it tonight and we can talk about it tomorrow." She got up from the table and muttered. "He has a brother. Didn't see that coming."

CHAPTER FIFTEEN

Max got in her dad's Mini Cooper and thought about what she planned to do. Nicholas was a suspect and she had to face the fact that he could be a murderer. It probably wasn't smart to be alone with a murder suspect, no matter how much she wanted answers. She called Olivia to find out if Quinn and Ashley were out with her. Maybe they hadn't gone out after all.

Olivia answered and Max heard the sounds of a noisy restaurant in the background. She was with Quinn and Ashley. Max thought about changing her plan to talk to Nicholas when Olivia mentioned that Zach was hanging out with him. Feeling safer, Max headed for the beach house.

When Nicholas answered the door, he seemed surprised to see her but quickly recovered and invited her in. Zach greeted her excitedly.

"Max!" He grinned at her, pulling her into a bear hug. "Thank you for looking out for Olivia while I was gone."

"That's what friends are for," Max said as he released her.

"The women are out to dinner together," Zach said as they walked to the living room.

"I know," Max said. "I thought I'd stop in and see you guys."

"Come on in," Nicholas said, heading for the living room. "We have some gourmet pizza left if you're hungry."

Max thought one piece of pizza couldn't hurt, but decided against it. If she kept eating the way she had been lately, she was going to have to go on a diet. And there were few things she hated more than diets. She also turned down the offer of a glass of wine. Nicholas pulled a bottle of water out of the refrigerator and handed it to her.

"Is this the first time you two have met?" Max sat down at one end of the sofa and Zach took the other end. Nicholas sat on the arm of one of the overstuffed chairs and sipped his wine.

"Yeah," Zach answered. "We figured we could get to know each other while the women were out. Why didn't you go with them, Max?"

Nicholas didn't look thrilled about having company, or maybe something else was bothering him. "I figured I'd let them catch up. With everything going on, they haven't had much chance to talk. Without me, they can tell all their college stories without worrying about boring me." Plus, they hadn't invited her. She tried not to feel put out about it.

"I figured the same thing," Zach said. "I got to meet Quinn and Ashley, and I thought I'd just hang out with Nicholas and let the women have some girl time."

Max wondered how she was going to bring up her questions. Subtlety was not always her strong suit.

"Nicholas has been telling me about his writing," Zach said. "Have you read his novels? They're fantastic."

"I just started reading *Immersion*. It's really wonderful. I had trouble putting it down. And don't either of you dare to tell me anything about the plot." Max was grateful that Zach had segued into the subject she wanted to talk about. "My dad told me that

Alfred had a brother before I got to that part in the book. I totally didn't see that coming."

Nicholas looked up from his wineglass and seemed more attentive than before but said nothing.

"Did you base the characters in your books on real people?" she asked.

She saw a flash of anger in his eyes. "It's fiction. Why don't people understand that concept?"

"Oh, I'm so sorry." Max said, not understanding where his anger was coming from. "I know nothing about writing."

Nicholas leaned back in his chair and stared out the window. They all sat in silence for several moments until Zach spoke.

"How are you enjoying Crystal Shores?" he asked Nicholas.

"I prefer to stay at home," he said, walking to the kitchen to refill his wine glass.

Max looked at Zach who just shrugged. "When do your parents arrive?" Zach had moved to California from Nebraska, and his parents still lived in the same house he grew up in.

"They'll be here Friday." Zach and Max made more small talk while Nicholas returned to the armchair. He morosely stared at the red wine in the glass he was quickly draining.

"I hope you can talk Olivia out of cancelling the wedding," Max said to Zach.

Nicholas perked up. "You guys are thinking of cancelling the wedding?"

"Not me," Zach said. "Olivia."

"I'm just ready to head back home," Nicholas said.

Max thought it was extremely selfish of Nicholas to want Zach and Olivia to cancel their wedding so he could leave town.

Or did he want to be as far as possible from the murder investigation?

Zach had a wistful look on his face. "I'm not sure if I'm going to be able to talk her out of it. She seems pretty determined, and you know how single minded she can be. As far as I'm concerned, I don't want to wait a single day longer to marry her. When I asked her to marry me, I tried to get her to elope. Did she tell you that, Max?"

"Yes." Max laughed. "She said you seemed to be in a big hurry, but she could never figure out why."

"Have you ever been so sure of something that you just know it's right and you don't want to wait?" Zach didn't wait for either of them to answer. "I fell in love with her at first sight, and after I talked her into marrying me, I wanted us to start our life together as soon as possible. Still do."

"Well, I'm on your side, Zach," Max said. "I managed to get her to put off the decision until you got back in town. Now it's your job to keep her from cancelling."

"I accept the challenge," Zach said looking hopeful. Max didn't see how Olivia could resist him and felt reassured that the wedding would go on as planned. After all, she knew how much Olivia had been looking forward to marrying Zach.

Nicholas didn't participate in the conversation. Max started to wonder what Quinn saw in him, but then he seemed livelier around her.

Zach and Max chatted some more, but with little hope that she'd learn anything else from Nicholas, Max finally said goodnight and drove home.

Her dad's lights were on tonight, and it made her feel safe just knowing he was there. She went up to her apartment and changed into her pajamas. She took a cup of tea and Nicholas's book to her room and climbed into bed, leaning back on a stack of pillows. Turning the book over, she stared at Nicholas's picture on the back cover as if it might tell her something. He looked carefree. Of course he had no idea what the future held.

Nicholas genuinely seemed tortured by his past. She couldn't imagine losing three family members at once. It had been nearly two years since she'd lost her mother and she still grieved her, but her death wasn't unexpected, coming at the end of a yearlong illness. Nicholas's life had been turned upside down in one day. No wonder he was still troubled by it.

She found her place in the book and started reading. Alfred, the main character, was an only child. At least Max had thought so until Richard mentioned his brother, spoiling a major plot point. His half brother had been given up for adoption years before Alfred was born, and he found out about him on his mother's deathbed. When he found his brother, he was surviving by any means necessary. Alfred convinced him to join him on his journey, but he disappointed him at every turn and they finally parted ways. Even after everything he put him through, he never stopped loving him.

Max closed the book. Nicholas said he hadn't based the characters in his novel on real people in his life, but was he just protecting his brother's memory? She was curious now and got out of bed to search the internet for information on Nicholas's brother. It took several tries, but she finally learned that his brother's name was Ian. She wasn't able to learn anything else about him, so she finally gave up and went back to bed.

Whatever the relationship was between Nicholas and Ian, it probably didn't have anything to do with the murder. But she couldn't stop thinking about it. Had Nicholas loved Ian the way that Alfred loved his brother? Had Ian been as big a disappointment? Max reminded herself that the book was a work of fiction as Nicholas had said. Alfred's brother might have been the product of Nicholas's imagination, nothing more.

She kept telling herself to put the book down and go to sleep, but kept reading until after two o'clock. She was not going to be happy with herself tomorrow when the alarm went off.

CHAPTER SIXTEEN

Max groaned when the alarm clock rang, but she dragged herself out of bed and got dressed. She might just as well have slept in since Detective Cruz was not at the beach that morning. She knew he must be putting in long hours at the station. After all, he was trying to solve a murder.

Max walked south along the shore until she could just make out the house where Olivia's friends were staying. What were they doing right now? Were they talking about the murder? It was possible they were all involved. None of them seemed to have fond feelings for Gabby, though Quinn seemed to pity her at least. But the question remained: Why would any of them want her dead? She stared out at the ocean lost in thought, but no answers came to her except for her suspicion that Nicholas had a secret. She turned to go home.

Walking back to the main beach, she noticed a man with shaggy hair wearing jeans and a tee shirt walking toward her. He stuck out since most people wore shorts on a sunny, warm morning like today. She glanced at his face, and she was sure he was the man from the sketch—the man that Nicholas had seen. Her pulse quickened as she told herself to stay calm.

Trying her best to be inconspicuous, she sat down on the beach and pretended to be engrossed in her phone. When he walked past her again, she got up and followed him at what she hoped was a safe distance. A short way later, he walked away from the water until he reached the steps that led up to the street.

At the top of the steps, Max looked around for the stranger. He was about a block away, heading north. She headed in his direction, thinking if she could just find out where he lived, she could report the information to Detective Cruz. A nagging voice told her this was a bad idea. After all, he could be a murderer. But if he were a murderer, he needed to be caught and put in jail. Not willing to let him get away with it, she kept following but slowed down to allow more space between them.

He turned down Zinnia Street, but by the time she got to the corner he was nowhere to be seen. She'd lost him. She walked a block down the street before she decided to give up. Maybe he lived on Zinnia Street. At least she could report that much information back to the police.

She turned to head back toward the beach and the man appeared on the sidewalk in front of her seemingly out of nowhere. She stopped breathing for a moment, panic coursing through her body.

"Why are you following me?" he demanded.

"What?" Max stood motionless with her heart pounding in her ears. She tried to think of what to tell him, but her mind was completely blank.

"You heard me," he snarled. "You've been following me since I left the beach."

"No, I haven't," she protested unconvincingly. "Why would I be following you?"

He stared at her as if trying to figure out the answer to her question. "Have you been talking to my ex? I told her she'd better leave me alone. First, she stalks me and now she's having me followed?"

"No," she stammered. "I don't know your ex. I'm just out for a walk."

She saw her old schoolteacher Mrs. Carpenter come out of her house with her poodle on a leash and felt a wave of relief. Not that the seventy year old woman was likely to protect her from a murderer, but surely he wouldn't do anything in broad daylight in front of a witness. At least she hoped he wouldn't. "Hello, Mrs. Carpenter," she called out and headed down the street to meet up with her. She could walk alongside Mrs. Carpenter until she was out of danger.

As they turned the corner, she turned back and saw the man staring after her. A small shiver went through her body. At Rose Street, she said goodbye to her old teacher and walked home.

She called Detective Cruz and left him a message, that she had seen the man from the sketch on Zinnia Street, leaving out the part about how she had followed him. Perhaps the police could go door to door on the street showing residents the sketch. At least it was a lead.

After a shower and a change of clothes, she sat across from her dad at his dining room table with her coffee and oatmeal. Her thoughts bounced around her head like a ball in a pinball machine.

"Penny for your thoughts," Richard said. "Although I suppose it should be at least a quarter by now with inflation."

She looked up at her dad and forced a smile. "Sorry, Dad. I guess I'm not very good company this morning." She wasn't about to tell him she had followed a possible murderer and he had confronted her. "Olivia's considering postponing her wedding. I couldn't wait for everyone to see her in her wedding gown, especially Zach. I know they'll still get married eventually, but I'm not sure if they're going to have the big wedding she'd planned. I don't even know if she'll wear the dress I designed."

"You never told me how it came out."

"It's amazing if I do say so myself. I'm prouder of it than any dress I've designed. Olivia seemed really pleased with it. You should have seen the way she glowed when she tried it on. Then Gabby showed up."

"Ah yes, Gabby. Poor girl. It's always sad when someone dies, but when they're as young as she was, it seems especially tragic. Have the police made any arrests yet?"

"No." Max stood up and took her half-eaten cereal to the sink and poured it down the garbage disposal. She didn't want to tell her dad that Olivia's friends were suspects. She didn't want him to worry about her any more than he did already. "I'd better get going. Want to go out to dinner tonight?"

"I can't tonight," he said.

She waited for him to elaborate, and when he didn't she asked, "Do you have a date? You can tell me, you know."

"I know. I guess you could call it a date, but it's really just dinner with a friend."

"Anyone I know?" She hoped she wasn't prying. He used to tell her everything, but he didn't talk much about his dating life to her.

Richard hesitated. "I don't think you know her."

"I know everyone, Dad."

"Don't exaggerate. You don't know everyone. It's Irena Newberg from my yoga class."

Max gasped. "But she's my age!"

His eyebrows rose with surprise. "How do you know Irena?"

"She got her wedding dress from our shop. Wait—is she still married?"

"Divorced. And for your information, she's not your age. She's in her mid-thirties." He seemed disappointed in her reaction.

"I wasn't— I mean, oh gosh. I'm sorry." She hung her head in guilt. Who was she to say whom her dad should or shouldn't date? Although, technically, at the age of fifty-eight he was old enough to be Irena's father. But that didn't matter as long as he was happy. "It's just hard to get used to the idea of you dating. Have a wonderful time tonight and I'll see you later." She hugged her dad and gave him a kiss on the cheek. "If you end up marrying her, don't expect me to call her Mom."

Richard laughed. "It's just dinner, Max. Don't get ahead of yourself."

CHAPTER SEVENTEEN

Max felt the need to spoil herself a little, so she stopped at Rose Street Cafe for a cappuccino. As she got her drink to go, she heard her name and turned to see Lori sitting at one of the tables. Max groaned inwardly. Why did she keep running into that woman? Maybe she'd just never noticed her before they'd met. Or maybe she'd just recently started hanging out in Crystal Shores. Had she spent the night with Jason? Max didn't even want to think about that. She gave a little wave, but Lori motioned her over.

"Hi, Lori," Max said. She was going to find a new place to get coffee in the future.

"Is there anything I should do to get ready for our appointment tomorrow?" Lori asked. "I really know nothing about wedding gowns. Should I do some research?"

"Just buy a few magazines and tear out pictures of the dresses you like. And bring shoes with the heel height you plan to wear for the wedding. I recommend a low heel. If you wear four inch heels on your wedding day your feet will be killing you by the end of the night."

"Great. Thanks for the tip."

"Okay, well I'll see you tomorrow."

By the time she got to work it was almost ten and Max wasn't in a good mood. When she turned the sign around to OPEN,

Keiko arrived, dressed in a plaid pleated skirt, white shirt, tie, and blazer.

"Good morning!" Max said, instantly cheered up by Keiko's presence. "What imaginary school do you attend?

Keiko rolled her eyes. "Lots of women in Japan wear outfits like this, not just schoolgirls."

"I see." One of the things Max looked forward to each day was seeing what Keiko would wear. Keiko didn't seem to be in the mood to be teased about her outfit, although Max had a feeling it would bother her more if she didn't comment. "You're early today. Did I ask you to come in early and forget?"

"No," Keiko laughed, "although that is something you would totally do. I thought you could use some help since you have a murder to solve. I hope you don't mind."

"No, not at all. I've told you before, you can work as many hours as you want while school's out for summer. I can always use the help, but I know you've got your website business, too. We really need to talk about hiring another assistant."

Keiko frowned. "I don't want to upset the delicate balance of our relationship."

Max laughed. "Well, I'd risk it if it meant I didn't have to work Sundays like I've been doing a lot lately. Want to share my cappuccino?"

"Thanks, but I have already had three cups of coffee this morning. I woke up early and could not get back to sleep trying to figure out who killed Gabby. Detective Cruz called me after we had brunch but I couldn't get any information out of him."

"Well, that's how it usually works," Max said with a smile. "The police are more interested in getting information than giving it out."

"We need to find out who killed her before Olivia's friends leave town. It will be harder after they leave, I think."

"You're probably right. But I'm not sure what to do next." Max sat down on the sofa, carefully removed the lid from her cup, and took a sip. "I saw the guy from the sketch this morning. At least I'm pretty sure it's the same guy."

Keiko stopped on her way to the office and spun around. "Really?" she gasped. "What did you do? Did you talk to him?"

"No, I did something equally as stupid," she admitted. "I followed him."

"You didn't! I'm not sure if that was stupid or brave. Did you find out where he lives?"

"No, he caught me following him and confronted me. He asked me why I was following him and I froze. I didn't know what to say. " She told Keiko about using her old teacher to make her escape. "I left Detective Cruz a message telling him I saw him on Zinnia Street. Hopefully that information is helpful."

"There's a halfway house on that street," Keiko said. "I bet that's where he lives."

"How do you know about a halfway house and I don't?" Sometimes, Keiko seemed to be a step ahead of her.

"I spent the morning researching people with criminal records in the area and I found out about it. The residents have been fighting to get rid of it. They don't like ex-cons living in their neighborhood."

"I can't say I blame them," Max said.

"They only accept non-violent offenders," Keiko said, putting her hands on her hips. "People deserve a second chance, don't they?"

"I suppose so," Max said, but was still uncomfortable about the idea of ex-cons in their neighborhood. It was much easier to be open minded about such things when it didn't directly affect you. "Well, it's in Detective Cruz's capable hands now. I don't see what else we can do."

"Research," Keiko said. As far as Keiko was concerned, research was the answer to almost any question. "And I already have a good start on it." She sat down across from Max and opened her laptop. "Maybe Gabby was killed by the man you saw this morning, but then what motive did he possibly have?"

"Maybe he was her drug connection," Max suggested, thinking he looked like he could be a drug dealer. Then she reminded herself that looks could be deceiving, and it was rarely a good idea to make assumptions based on appearance. "Although that would be bad for business, I suppose."

"True," Keiko said. "I think drug dealers do not usually kill off their customers."

"Do you think one of Olivia's friends is a more likely suspect? What would their motive be after not seeing her for eight years? Remember what you overheard the night Gabby was murdered? That she knew the truth about Nicholas?"

"Maybe we should be focusing on Nicholas. We already know he lost his family in a fire. Check out the newspaper article about it." She turned the laptop around so Max could read it.

Max stared at the pictures of Nicholas, his brother, and their parents. It said Nicholas escaped the fire that killed his brother and parents. He leapt out of a second story window, injuring himself in the fall, but his family was trapped by the flames. By the time firefighters arrived, it was too late for them. The fire started on the first floor where his brother was sleeping. It was suspicious, but the arson investigators never found out who'd set the blaze.

"It's so sad," Max said quietly. The picture of Nicholas was the same one from the back of his book from when he had shoulder length hair and a full beard. He looked every bit the artist. He had a big grin as if he didn't have a care in the world, and Max wondered if he ever smiled like that these days. She looked at the picture of his brother, which was somewhat blurry as if it had been blown up from a snapshot. "Nicholas looks so different now. I mean besides shaving his head and his beard. It's like he lost his innocence. I don't know how you get over a tragedy like that."

"It would have to change you," Keiko agreed. "He seems almost haunted now, doesn't he?"

"He seems different than the happy guy in the picture. I don't know if haunted is the right word." A thought occurred to Max. "You don't suppose Nicholas set the fire, do you?" She shook her head. "No, that's too awful to even think about."

"But possible," Keiko said. "The article does say the cause of the fire was suspicious."

"Why would a successful author kill his entire family?" Max slumped down on the sofa, unable to shake the idea from her mind. "But maybe it was accidental. He seems almost guilty when he talks about them. Olivia did say he had survivor's guilt. I guess that can happen when you're happy to be alive and then feel bad about being happy."

"This may not cheer you up," Keiko said. "The Crystal Shores Police have increased their online security and I was unable to learn anything about the investigation."

"Well, good. I don't think it's a good idea for you to be hacking into the police database. What if you were caught?" Max had suspected before that Keiko used her hacking skills to get information, but this was the first time she'd admitted it.

"I am very careful. Anyway, the coroner's office doesn't have the same level of security, so I was able to find out that Gabby's alcohol blood level was three times the legal limit. They also found Zolpidem in her system."

"Zolpidem?" Max forgot for a moment to scold Keiko.

"It's a sleeping pill," Keiko said. "And it would explain why she didn't struggle."

"Why would Gabby take a sleeping pill before she went to lie on the beach? Especially after drinking all that vodka."

"Maybe it wasn't hers," Keiko said. "Maybe someone slipped it to her. They could have put it in her drink."

"That's an interesting thought. I wonder if any of Olivia's friends had a subscription for Zolpidem."

"That I wasn't able to find out," Keiko said. "But I bet Detective Cruz knows. I wish I could find out more. I know someone who might be able to get me into their system."

Max looked at Keiko sternly. "You've got to stop this, Keiko. You could get into real trouble."

Keiko sighed. "Someone's been murdered, Max. I have done things in my past that I'm not proud of, stupid stuff, but I'm not going to apologize for helping solve a murder."

Max wondered what sorts of things sweet, innocent-seeming Keiko had done. Maybe that was why she always seemed nervous when Detective Cruz was around.

Keiko went into the office, and Max didn't ask her what she was working on. Hopefully she took her warning seriously and wasn't trying to hack into the police department's computers or get someone else to do it for her.

CHAPTER EIGHTEEN

In spite of the murder, Max still had a business to run. The first appointment of the day arrived at noon. Yasminda Silva was getting married next spring and was coming in with her mother, sister and best friend to try on wedding gowns. Olivia had referred Yasminda who she had hired to replace her as resident stage manager for the Crystal Shores Playhouse when she'd taken over as artistic director. The previous artistic director, Kenneth, was Darlene's husband and they had both decided to retire last summer.

The moment the four women arrived, they were chattering loudly, asking Max questions and generally creating chaos.

Yasminda was the most casually dressed of the group, wearing jeans and a tank top. Her dark hair was swept into a loose bun on top of her head. "Poor Olivia." She said. "She has been a wreck. I told her she should just take the week off. Our show closes on Friday and we're pretty much on automatic pilot at this point."

"Olivia's too responsible to take off work unless she's on her death bed," Max said.

"Boy, that's the truth. She comes to work before anyone else and she's always the last to leave. She's so dedicated to her job, which is great, but, you know, there's a limit. Did she tell you she's thinking of cancelling her wedding because of what happened?"

"Well, I don't blame her," Mrs. Silva said. "Who wants to get married on the same beach where a murder took place?"

The bride-to-be ignored this comment, and handed Max pictures of sleek gowns. Her sister Anna and her friend Charlotte started pawing through the wedding gowns hung on one side of the shop, pulling out dresses and calling out to Yasminda.

"Look at this one, Yasminda!" Anna called out. "It's sexy. Robby's eyes will pop out of his head if you wear this one."

"Don't listen to her," Charlotte said. "This one looks like something Beyoncé would wear. Try this one on!"

Max clearly was not in control.

"Okay, ladies," she said firmly. "How about we do this one at a time? Mrs. Silva, let me have those pictures you brought."

Yasminda's mother handed over the magazine pages she'd collected. She clearly wanted her daughter to look like Cinderella. "She should look like a princess," she said.

"I agree," Max said with a smile. "Now, Anna, what's most important to you?"

"My sister's gorgeous. Just look at her," Anna said, and Yasminda blushed. "I don't want tons of fabric covering up her sexy body. There definitely should be cleavage."

"No cleavage," Mrs. Silva said. "It's not appropriate for church."

"Mom," Yasminda said in a voice only a daughter used to getting her way can use, "I told you I want to get married on the beach."

"After what happened?" Mrs. Silva said in a shocked voice. "You can't possibly--"

"Okay," Max interrupted gently. She didn't want to get in the middle of an argument about the venue now. "We'll figure out the cleavage thing later. What about you, Charlotte?" She needed to get control if it was even possible at this point, or else this was going to take all day.

"It's gotta have bling," Charlotte said.

"Got it. Princess, sexy, bling. Should we ask what Yasminda wants?"

The three women stared at Max for a moment as if it had just occurred to them that Yasminda might have an opinion. "Of course," her mother finally said.

"Great," Max said. "So, what is most important to you for your wedding gown, Yasminda? I'm sure you've been dreaming of this day for a long time, or at least since you met Robby."

Yasminda giggled. "I want Robby to take one look at me and lose his mind."

"Okay, got it. Princess, sexy, bling, lose his mind." She took the two dresses from Anna and Charlotte and picked out a princess style dress, which she showed to Mrs. Silva for her approval.

"But—" Yasminda began, but Max held up one finger.

"Keiko, take everyone into the Dream Room and let Yasminda try on these three dresses." She turned to the bride-to-be. "I don't want you to make any decisions until after you've tried on at least four dresses, no matter what anyone says. Understand?"

Max and Yasminda had had a long talk before she came into the shop. She told Max about her domineering family, and Max had asked her to trust her. Yasminda hesitated for a moment, then nodded and followed Keiko into the other room.

With most brides, Max would pick out the perfect dress and have them try it on. A few brides needed to try on several others before they realized that Max had made the right choice. But sometimes, she needed a different approach, and this was one of those times. Yasminda needed to try on three wrong dresses so that she and her family would recognize the right one when they saw it.

Max closed her eyes and mentally reviewed their entire inventory of gowns. Her eyes popped open. She knew just the dress that would make everyone happy, most importantly, Yasminda. She climbed the stairs to the upper floor and found it.

Sitting down in the showroom holding what she hoped was the perfect dress, Max found she enjoyed listening to the chattering coming from the other room as long as she didn't have to be smack in the middle of it. The women laughed and argued, then laughed some more.

Keiko came out of the Dream Room and plopped down next to Max. "Your turn," she said. "They wore me out. Go work your miracle."

Max took Yasminda back to the dressing room while the other three women had a heated discussion about which dress she should get. She helped the bride-to-be into the dress she'd picked out and watched her face light up as she saw herself in the mirror. Max led her out into the Dream Room and smiled as she saw Mrs. Silva's jaw drop. Anna and Charlotte silently watched as Yasminda climbed up on the pedestal.

The off the shoulder neckline showed just a touch of cleavage and the bodice accentuated Yasminda's hourglass figure down to her hips where it flared out in yards of chiffon.

Mrs. Silva started to cry, which was something Max was used to. Anna hugged her sister and told her that Robbie would definitely lose his mind.

Max gave Keiko a look and tapped her head. Keiko apparently understood and left the room. Only Charlotte looked unhappy.

"Where's the bling?" she asked.

Keiko reappeared with a crystal-encrusted tiara that looked like it belonged on Queen Elizabeth. She placed it on top of Yasminda's head.

Charlotte grinned. "Perfect!" she cried out.

Keiko leaned over to Max. "See?" she whispered. "You are a miracle worker."

oOo

Keiko had just returned from the deli with lunch for both of them when the door jingled and a thirty-something woman with shoulder length brown hair entered.

"Hello," Max greeted her. "I'm Max and this is Keiko. How can we help you?"

"I hope you can," the woman said in a worried voice. "I'm getting married a week from Saturday, and I've been to four different bridal shops. None of them could help."

"Let me guess. You ordered your dress from Antoine's Bridal," Max said.

"Yes. I'm desperate. I've even tried buying one online, but by the time it got here there wouldn't be time for alterations if I needed them."

Max took a long look at the bride-to-be. 5'6" 155-160 pounds. She was dressed very conservatively in tan slacks and a white long sleeved shirt. She reminded her of someone.

"Would you consider borrowing a dress?" Max had a very specific dress in mind.

"At this point, I'd consider anything," the woman said.

Max got on the phone and called Susan Brown, asking if she would consider loaning her dress to a bride in crisis. Susan said she'd be right over.

"I've completely forgotten my manners," the woman said, smiling for the first time since she arrived. "My name's Alice."

Max put on a pot of tea and they chatted while they waited for Susan. They didn't have to wait long.

Susan arrived with her dress. Max helped her take it out of the plastic garment bag it was in and Susan proudly showed off her gown. "What do you think?" Susan asked Alice.

"Oh my," Alice gushed. "It's gorgeous. Are you sure you want someone else wearing it?"

"I would love nothing better than someone to wear it on their wedding day," Susan said. "It seems a shame that such a beautiful dress only gets worn once. I just hope it fits."

Max had Alice into the dress in no time. It fit like a glove, which was a relief since Max didn't want to make any alterations on Susan's dress. Max, Keiko, and Susan watched while Alice got up on the pedestal and saw herself in the mirror. She burst into tears.

Max shoved a box of tissues at Alice, but she ignored her and jumped off the pedestal to hug Susan. The two women were laughing and talking and Max and Keiko decided to leave them alone while they bonded.

When Alice left with the dress, Max invited Susan to join them for a cup of tea. Susan had a big grin on her face. "You made my day, Max," she said. "Now I see why you love your job so much. It's wonderful to make someone so happy."

"You are a hero," Keiko said. "You saved the day."

"No…" Susan began, shaking her head, and then looked at Keiko who nodded and smiled. "Okay, maybe. A little bit. I'm just glad I could help. Do you know she invited me to her wedding?"

Max refilled her teacup. "Are you going?"

"I don't think so," Susan said. "It would be too surreal seeing someone else walk down the aisle in my wedding gown. But we did exchange emails and she promised to send me pictures. She does look beautiful in my dress."

"Not as beautiful as you did," Max said and Keiko agreed.

After Susan left, Max and Keiko talked about how they could help the other brides. Another one called and Keiko got her information, too. That made five brides so far who needed dresses.

"We could have a small, private sample sale on Saturday," Max said. "Is that a crazy idea?"

"Only a little crazy," Keiko said. "I mean, we didn't make any appointments for Saturday. How much time do we really need to get ready for the wedding?"

"I suppose we could gather a couple of dozen dresses," Max said. Maybe it wasn't such a crazy idea. And if it helped some desperate brides save their dream weddings, then it would be worth it. "We'll have a lot of alterations work to do, but most of the brides aren't getting married right away." She thought about all the work involved, but there were brides that needed her help. "Let's do it," she decided. "Would you mind emailing everyone?"

"I will do it right now," Keiko said.

CHAPTER NINETEEN

Quinn called the shop to ask Max what time she and her sister should stop by to have their bridesmaid dresses hemmed. Max told her to stop on by now.

An hour later when Quinn and Ashley arrived, Max asked, "How do the dresses fit?"

"Mine's a little loose around the middle," Ashley said. "I like my dresses a little more fitted. Do you think you can take it in?"

"You bet," Max assured her. She took the two women back to the dressing rooms and they both changed into their bridesmaid's dresses. The gowns were simple floor length dresses with spaghetti straps that Max planned to wear more than once. Quinn's and Ashley's dresses were light silvery blue while Max's was a darker shade of cobalt. Olivia had asked Max to pick out the dresses, trusting her experience and fashion sense. Max felt that the bridesmaids shouldn't upstage the bride and wanted to make sure all eyes were on Olivia on her special day.

Max had sewn the bridesmaid's dresses since she wasn't happy with the shades of blue available for off the rack dresses, but she hadn't gotten around to sewing her own. She'd been too busy with Olivia's gown and Quinn's and Ashley's dresses.

After Ashley tried on her dress, Max had her take it off and put it back on inside out so she could pin the seams and make it more fitted. Ashley was slender, so she could get away with a dress that hugged her body. Max preferred a slightly looser fit since she didn't want to have to wear any slimming undergarments. Besides, she wanted to eat as much cake as she wanted on the big day. Once she finished with Ashley's dress, she helped Quinn into hers while Ashley changed back into her clothes.

"At least the weather has been lovely while you've been here," Max commented as she pinned up the hem of Quinn's bridesmaid dress. "Not that that makes up for what's happened, of course." Max felt stupid mentioning the weather, as if that mattered at all after their friend had been murdered. Besides, the weather was pretty much always nice in Crystal Shores if you didn't mind the typically overcast mornings.

"I've been trying to keep a positive attitude with the wedding coming up," Quinn said. "I don't want Gabby's death to put too much of a damper on Olivia's special day."

"I'd just reschedule the whole thing if I were her," Ashley said. "I don't think everyone's going to just forget about the murder by Saturday. I mean, is it even appropriate to have a big party after someone's just been murdered?"

Max said nothing. It was hard to keep quiet, but she didn't want to divulge that Olivia was considering cancelling the wedding. It was up to Olivia when and if she wanted to tell her friends. Max was still holding out hope that she would go through with it.

"Ashley," Quinn said, "you've never planned a wedding. It's not that easy to just reschedule. At this late date, they would lose thousands of dollars in deposits. And then they've got the honeymoon planned and booked. The whole schedule at the theater is arranged around Olivia taking time off. Besides, if there ever was a time that we need something positive in our lives, it's now."

"This must be really hard on both of you," Max said.

"It's never easy losing a friend," Quinn said. "But for her to be murdered was such a shock. I can't believe I'll never see her again."

Ashley looked down at her shoes. "I guess cancelling the wedding wouldn't bring Gabby back anyway."

"No, it wouldn't," Quinn agreed. "We've just got to help Olivia forget about all the ugliness so she can have her dream wedding. I can't wait to see the dress you've designed for her, Max."

"That's right," Max said. "You haven't seen it yet." She smiled, remembering seeing Olivia glowing in the gown she'd created before she even knew Gabby was in town. Was that just a few days ago? Things could change so quickly and without any warning. "It's really beautiful, if I do say so myself. Olivia is going to look gorgeous."

"Have you seen what the ushers are wearing?" Quinn asked.

"They've got it easy," Max laughed. "Men always do, don't they? They're wearing matching Hawaiian shirts."

"Nicholas is wearing a Hawaiian shirt, too, since the invitation said the dress code was casual," Quinn said.

"So's my dad. He had plenty in his closet, but he thought it was a good excuse to go out and buy another one."

Max finished pinning up the hem of Quinn's dress and sent her back to the dressing room to change. "I'll wait for you in the showroom," Max said. She turned to Ashley. "Would you like some tea or do you have to rush off?"

"Nicholas is picking us up," Ashley said, following Max into the showroom. "He should be here pretty soon."

"Well, I'll make a pot of tea anyway while we're waiting," Max said. Keiko followed her to the office.

"I'm going to get back to work on the website, if that's okay," Keiko said.

"Sure. I'll be out of your hair in a minute."

"Max?" Ashley called out.

"What is it?" Max came out of the office. Ashley was staring at the front door.

"There's a cat pawing at your door," Ashley said.

"Oh, that's just Josie," Max said, opening the door. "She's the shop cat at the yarn store next door." The sleek black cat sauntered in and walked past the two of them, then jumped up onto an armchair and curled up. "What are you doing here, Josie? Were Fiona and Teresa ignoring you?"

"She acts like she owns the place," Quinn said, laughing as she came out from the dressing room.

"Yes, she does. She's pretty special so we let her get away with a lot." She reached down and scratched Josie behind one ear.

"What's so special about her?" Ashley asked. "She looks like an ordinary black cat."

Josie raised her head and Max could have sworn she gave Ashley a disdainful look before she put her head back down and closed her eyes.

"Well," Max said, "for one thing, she brought Teresa and Simon together. Teresa owns the yarn shop next door with her sister. One day Josie showed up at their door and Teresa fell in love with her. She put up signs all over town and that's how she met Simon, Josie's owner. They've been dating ever since."

Josie started purring loudly.

"That's sweet," Quinn said.

"And you think the cat is some sort of a matchmaker?" Ashley asked. "I think it's just a coincidence. A lucky coincidence, sure, but a coincidence just the same."

"Maybe the cat could find someone for you, Ashley," Quinn said with a smirk.

"Right," Ashley said sarcastically. "I'm not that desperate."

"Not yet," Quinn said, and Ashley slugged her arm. "Ow!"

Max left the two sisters to their good-natured bickering and went into the office to fix the tea. She returned with the teapot and three teacups. While she was pouring the tea, Nicholas arrived.

"Hi, ladies," he said, as if he were making an effort to sound cheerful. Max had gotten used to his bored manner and was surprised to see him trying to be upbeat.

Josie jumped off the sofa, arched her back, and hissed loudly at him.

"Josie!" Max said. "What's gotten into you?"

Josie ran past Nicholas toward the door. Max dashed to the door and let the cat out.

"Well, that was odd," Max said. She'd never seen Josie act that way.

"Maybe she doesn't like men," Quinn suggested. "I had a dog like that once. He used to growl at any strange man that came to the house."

"I remember that dog," Nicholas said. "It hated me."

"Yeah, maybe that's it," Max said, thinking Josie seemed to tolerate Simon just fine. But then, Simon had owned Josie since she was a kitten.

"Ready to go?" Nicholas asked Quinn.

"But Max just made a pot of tea," Quinn said, looking at Max apologetically.

"That's okay," Max said. "I can drink a whole pot by myself. No worries."

Quinn gave her a hug while Ashley stood by with her arms crossed and Nicholas opened the front door. He seemed to be in a hurry to get out of there. After they left, Max wondered if he were hiding something. He seemed like the most likely one to kill Gabby considering that they had words the night of the murder. Was he hiding the fact that he was a murderer or did he have a different secret?

Chapter Twenty

Teresa entered the bridal shop with a huge smile on her face and holding Josie in her arms. Josie seemed a little skittish at first and looked around the shop. Was she checking to see if Nicholas was still there?

"Hello, Teresa," Max said. "Hello again, Josie," she said to the cat and scratched it behind the ears. "You can relax. Nicholas is gone."

"She's been sneaking out lately," Teresa said, "so I'm keeping a close eye on her. She'll slip out when a customer opens the door and she dashes away so fast I can't find her. So far she always comes back after a few minutes, but I worry about her. There's so much traffic on Coast Highway."

"She came and visited us earlier," Max said. "Does she dislike men?"

"Well," Teresa said, thinking, "she tolerates Simon, but he's owned her since she was a kitten. She's not really around a lot of other men. We don't get many men in the yarn shop. Why do you ask?"

"She really didn't like Nicholas," Max said. "He's one of Olivia's friends who came down from San Francisco for the wedding."

"I wouldn't read too much into it," Teresa said. "She's a finicky cat to say the least."

Keiko came out from the office and said hello, giving Teresa a hug.

Teresa looked very happy about something, and Max had an idea she knew what it was. "You look like you have good news. Spill. I could use cheering up."

"Is it that obvious?" Teresa asked. "I'm not supposed to tell anyone. I mean with everything going on, we didn't think it was the right time." Josie squirmed and jumped out of Teresa's arms. The cat began to investigate the room, sniffing at the hems of the wedding dresses and walking back toward the office.

Keiko clapped her hands gleefully. "He proposed, didn't he?"

Max had just come to the same conclusion, and Teresa didn't need to say a word. "Let's see the ring."

Teresa held out her hand, showing them a lovely Art Deco style white gold engagement ring with a diamond that was just the right size for the setting, probably a half-carat or so. It was perfect for Teresa, who was very old fashioned, unlike her more modern sister, Fiona.

"I've been waiting for this day." Max grabbed Teresa in a hug. When she'd released her, it was Keiko's turn for a hug.

"When's the wedding?" Keiko asked.

"We haven't set a date yet. We don't want to wait too long, but I know you need a few months to order my wedding gown."

Max grinned. "Would you like to try on lots of dresses or would you like to see the one I've already picked out for you?"

"You've picked out a dress? Did Simon tell you he was going to propose?"

"No," Max said, "but anyone would be an idiot if they didn't see it coming. So, what do you think? It's your first wedding, so if you want to try on lots of dresses, I'm fine with that. It'll be fun." One of her favorite things was when a bride came in to try on wedding gowns. It was such an exciting occasion for a bride-to-be and Max loved being a part of choosing the perfect gown for the big day.

Keiko was ready to pull whatever dresses Max suggested, but Teresa shook her head, smiling knowingly. "At my age, I'd look ridiculous in most of these gowns. Just show me the one you picked out. I'll no doubt end up with it anyway."

"Great!" Max ran up the stairs to the second floor where she kept overflow inventory and special orders. She pulled a dress down from the rack and took the plastic off of it.

"Close your eyes," Max called down. At the bottom of the stairs, she giggled when she saw that Keiko had her eyes closed, too. When she stood in front of Teresa, she said, "Okay, you can open them now. Both of you."

Teresa and Keiko gasped in unison. The ivory dress was empire style with long sleeves and a square neckline, almost Regency in style. The entire dress was covered in embroidered chiffon over a silk underdress. The chiffon was light and airy as gossamer.

Josie walked over to the dress, sniffed the air around it, and started purring loudly. She rubbed up against Max's legs.

"I guess Josie approves," Max said, smiling.

Max took Teresa into the dressing room and helped her into the dress. Once she stood on the platform of the Dream Room with six mirrors reflecting her image, Teresa looked as lovely as any young blushing bride.

"You look beautiful!" Keiko said. "May I go get Fiona?"

Soon Keiko held the door while Fiona hobbled in on crutches with an orthopedic boot on one foot.

"Fiona, what happened to you?" Max ran over to help but Fiona shooed her away.

"Teresa didn't tell you what her cat did to me this morning?" Fiona said in an indignant tone.

"Not a thing," Max said and Keiko nodded.

"I stepped out the back door to take some trash across the alley to the dumpster and Josie slipped out the door and tripped me. I sprained my ankle. Now I've got to wear this stupid boot and walk around on crutches."

"Now, now, tell them the rest," Teresa prodded.

Fiona sighed. "Just after I fell, a car came speeding down the alley."

"Fiona might have been killed!" Teresa said.

Fiona gave her sister a sideways glance. "That's a little dramatic, don't you think?"

"No," Teresa said. "I don't. I think Josie is a hero. She may have saved your life."

"By tripping me?"

"Yes," Teresa said. "If she hadn't, you would have been in the alley when the car raced by."

"I just wish she could have figured out a way to save my life without me ending up with a sprained ankle. These crutches are a pain in the--"

"You are alive," Keiko said. "That is the important thing."

"Yes," Max agreed. "I'm very glad you weren't more seriously hurt. A sprained ankle will heal fairly quickly. I'm sorry you have to walk on crutches though. It does make getting around difficult."

"Okay, enough about my ankle and the amazing Josie, let me get a good look at my sister."

Max was surprised to see Teresa's practical, no-nonsense sister fighting back tears.

"You're a vision," Fiona said, and a tear finally escaped and rolled down her cheek. Max shoved a box of tissues at her and Fiona took one, looking embarrassed by her show of emotion. "Simon is a very lucky man."

"I'm the one who's lucky." Teresa grinned and did a little waltz, the skirt of the gown swinging back and forth. "I gave up on finding love a long time ago and then Josie came along and brought me Simon."

"She's just a cat, you know," Fiona said. "Just a regular, everyday black cat." As if on cue, Josie walked up to Fiona and rubbed against her legs.

"There's nothing regular or everyday about Josie," Teresa said sternly. "And don't try to convince me you're not attached to her, too. I see you sneaking her treats when you think I'm not looking."

Max laughed at the sisters' friendly quarreling. "I'm still waiting for your opinion," Max said to Teresa. "Would you like to try more dresses on?"

Teresa's glow said everything Max needed to know, but she still wanted to hear the words.

"It's perfect, Max," Teresa said. "You've done it again."

"It's her special power," Keiko said and everyone agreed. Max had a way of finding the perfect gown for any bride.

"I'd better get back to the shop. I was so excited I didn't lock up." She hugged her sister and hobbled to the door, struggling to open it. Keiko ran over to help.

"I'm fine," Fiona grumbled. "I'm not a helpless old lady who needs help."

"Of course not," Keiko said. "I'm not helping because you are an old lady, which you certainly are not. I am helping because you are on crutches."

"Fine," Fiona said and headed back to the Knitpickers.

Olivia called out from the front room, and Max called back, "We're in here."

Olivia stepped through the door of the Dream Room and stopped in her tracks. "Teresa! Look how beautiful you look! So he finally proposed."

Teresa's smile lit up her whole face. "Was I the only one who was surprised?"

Olivia laughed. "We saw it coming a mile away," she admitted. "The dress is lovely. Is this the one?"

"Yes, Max has done it again," Teresa said. "I don't know why I expected anything different. I just couldn't imagine what kind of dress would be right for me at my age. Luckily Max already had it figured out."

"I will help Teresa change so you two can talk," Keiko offered.

"What's up?" Max asked Olivia once they were alone in the front room.

Olivia looked stressed out, which was no surprise. "Zach and I have talked it over and I finally convinced him to postpone the wedding."

"Oh, no," Max said. "I'm so sorry to hear that. Are you sure?" She knew how much Olivia wanted to marry Zach, and she hoped she wouldn't regret the decision later.

"I couldn't have my wedding on the same beach where Gabby was murdered," Olivia said.

"Then have it somewhere else," Max suggested.

"Where in the world would I find a place to hold a wedding at the last minute? Some venues are booked a year in advance."

"So have it in our back yard."

"Your back yard would hold about ten people. It wouldn't even fit our families and the wedding party."

Max tried to think of another solution. "Well, then, someone else's back yard. You must know someone with enough room for a hundred people."

"The decision's been made, Max." Olivia sounded determined. Max knew when she heard that tone of voice that it was useless to argue.

Max sighed in defeat. "I wish you wouldn't, but of course it's your decision."

"I have a favor to ask you," Olivia said in a pleading voice. "I'm sorry to be such a burden."

"Don't be silly. Nothing you could ask would be a burden. You're my best friend and besides, I'm your maid of honor. What do you need?"

"I need to call all the vendors and cancel everything. I'm sure I'll lose my deposits, but that's just the way it is. I'm just dreading making those calls. I'm afraid I'll start crying again. I've cried enough for a while."

"Let me help," Max said. "I call vendors all the time, and my schedule is clear for the rest of the day. I was going to work on my bridesmaid dress, but I guess I don't need to do that now. Where's your list?"

Olivia reached in her purse, handed Max a folded piece of paper, and followed her to the office. She looked at the list of vendors: the bakery, the caterer, the DJ—the list went on and on.

The first phone call Max made was to Olivia's florist, which was Eric, owner of Flower to the People. As soon as she mentioned Olivia was with her and she was cancelling her wedding, he hung up on her. She sat there confused.

"What was that about?" Olivia asked.

"I have no idea," Max said, looking at the next name on the list. It was the bakery owned by the parents of her childhood crush, Andy. She decided to procrastinate and make that call later. If Andy answered, it might not be a quick phone call since they hadn't talked in a while. And it would probably be awkward, even after all this time.

She was about to call the caterer when she heard the front door jingle. Eric appeared at the office door and grabbed Olivia, giving her a long hug.

"Hi, Max," he said, though he was clearly thinking more about Olivia at that moment, which was okay with Max. "Now, Olivia. What do you have planned for the next two hours?"

"Max and I are calling the vendors," she said. "I want to call them all today. Then I need to contact all the guests."

"Max can take care of the vendors without you, can't you Max?" he asked.

"I've got it covered," Max assured him. "Just leave it to me."

"Good. I'm taking you to the spa," Eric said, taking Olivia by the hand.

"But—" she started to protest.

"No buts," he insisted. "A nice massage and maybe a facial and you'll be feeling much better." Before Olivia had a chance to protest further, he pulled her out the door as she said a quick goodbye to Max.

Keiko and Teresa emerged from the dressing room. Teresa gave both of them long hugs before she left.

"I overheard you from the next room," Keiko confessed. "Your friend Eric can be very domineering."

"Yes," Max said. "But in the very best way."

The front door jingled again and Zach appeared. "Where's Olivia?"

Max explained that Eric had taken her to the spa. "How are you doing?"

"How am I doing?" he echoed. "A woman I've never met has been murdered, my fiancé is mourning her, and my wedding is off."

"Okay, I suppose that was a stupid question," Max said.

"Sorry," he said. "I'm just a bit frazzled. Olivia said you were going to help her cancel the vendors. Do you have the list?"

"Yes," Max said. "Let me get it for you." She returned with the list. "But I don't mind making the calls. You must have a lot to do."

"I'll take care of the vendors," he said. "But don't tell Olivia, okay? Would you tell her you cancelled all of them?"

Max didn't like lying to Olivia and she told him so.

"Please?" he begged.

"Alright. What are you up to?"

"I just wanted to help. Olivia didn't want to dump everything on me, but I don't mind doing it. I'll make the calls, and she doesn't need to know."

Max looked at him skeptically, but she trusted him enough to give him the benefit of the doubt.

CHAPTER TWENTY-ONE

At closing time, Max's stomach grumbled. There was nothing to eat at home and her dad had plans. She asked Keiko, "Do you want to get some dinner with me?"

"Oh," Keiko said. "I have plans tonight."

"Is it a date?" Max asked. Keiko didn't talk about her love life much, in fact not at all. Max couldn't help but be curious.

"I'm just getting together with a friend," Keiko said evasively.

"Well, that's nice," Max said, resisting the urge to ask more questions. "I can finish up here if you want to head out."

"Thank you!" Keiko said, grabbed her things, and rushed out the door.

After running the floor duster around the shop and vacuuming the rug, Max locked the front door of Wedding Belles Bridal Shop and stood on the sidewalk wondering what to do for dinner. Her dad was out with Irena, and there was nothing in her apartment that would suffice for a meal. The Quick Fox was right across the street. They had great food and Burt, her favorite bartender, often knew a lot about what was going on in this town. Maybe he'd heard something about the murder. She didn't have any other leads to follow right now, so she headed to the crosswalk and waited for a break in traffic.

The Quick Fox had been in business for decades and served the best steaks in town. They were also known for their nightlife, with music five nights a week. By nine o'clock, many of the young, single men and women in town would arrive and stay until after midnight hoping to meet someone or just looking to enjoy a good time with friends. Max was usually in her pajamas by nine, usually curled up with a good book.

She found a seat at the bar and Burt handed her a glass of Chardonnay and a plate with olives, which he knew she loved. She ordered a shrimp cocktail which arrived quickly. Six enormous shrimp were perched on a martini glass full of cocktail sauce.

The music didn't start until much later, but the bar was nearly full and Burt was busy refilling glasses and mixing specialty drinks. Max was starting to wonder if she would have a chance to find out if he'd heard any gossip when Eric sat down next to her.

"Eric!" Max leaned in to give him air kisses, which he returned. "How was the spa day?"

"Wonderful," he gushed. "I had a hot stone massage and a facial. I feel positively rejuvenated."

"And Olivia?" She raised her eyebrows. "I thought the whole point was to make her feel better."

He scowled at her. "Is there a rule that says you can't enjoy yourself while cheering up a friend?" He caught Burt's eye and ordered a scotch on the rocks. "Olivia was as relaxed as a bowl of noodles by the time they were done with her."

"Well, that's good. Are you having dinner at the bar, too?"

"Just a drink while I wait for Jonathan. We'll be eating in the dining room."

She was a little disappointed she wouldn't have him to keep her company. "Oh, I see. Is he working late again?"

Eric grimaced. "He's a slave to that job. Sometimes we don't eat dinner until nine o'clock."

"Trouble in paradise?"

Eric laughed. "No. If the worst complaint I have about him is that he works too hard, I think that's pretty good, don't you? Besides, only old people eat dinner this early." He gave her a sideways glance. "Old people and you."

"I get too hungry to wait until seven or eight for dinner," Max said, taking a sip of her wine and eyeing her shrimp hungrily.

"Go ahead and eat," Eric said, and Max took a big bite of one of the shrimp with a generous dollop of cocktail sauce. "I suppose you've come to find out if Burt has heard anything."

Max swallowed and tried to look innocent. "Would you like a shrimp?" she asked, and Eric eyed her suspiciously. "Okay, fine. You know me so well. He's been too busy to talk, but I'm not sure how much he would know anyway. All the suspects and the victim were from out of town."

"I thought a stranger surprised her on the beach," Eric said. "That's what I've heard."

"It's a possibility, but I don't think that's what happened. I found her ring on the beach this morning. I can't think of any other reason a stranger would murder her besides theft, and she didn't have anything else of value. But then, I can't come up with a motive for Quinn, Nicholas or Ashley to kill her either." Max added in a whisper, "But we found out she had sleeping pills in her system."

Eric's eyes got wide. "Do you think they were hers? Or did someone slip them to her somehow?"

Max shook her head. "I don't know. But why would she voluntarily take sleeping pills on top of three martinis when she was going to lie on the beach? Detective Cruz won't tell me anything. I got angry with him because he had Olivia on his suspect list."

"Did you two have a falling out?" Eric asked. "You haven't even managed to get anything going with him and now you're on the outs?"

"I couldn't help it. Besides, there's not going to be anything between me and him. He's got a girlfriend, remember? The one with the perfect hair and perfect everything else."

"You really hate her, don't you?" Eric guessed.

"What? No. I don't even know her. She may be a very nice person." She crumbled under Eric's stare. "Fine, I hate her. I know it's completely irrational. It's just that she was so condescending. She said I was adorable."

"No! How could she!" Eric said in mock indignation. "What a horrible person."

Max laughed in spite of herself. "You weren't there. It was the way she said it, like I was a stray kitten or something."

"So how long are you going to stay mad at Detective Cruz?"

"I'm only hurting myself, so I suppose I should apologize. Even then I don't think he's going to share information."

"Maybe you don't need him to," Eric said with a gleam in his eye. "You know Tiffany Kearns, don't you?"

"Of course. Keiko designed her dress and we went to her wedding. You did her flowers, right?"

"Yep. She's working at the police station."

"You're kidding!" Max grinned. How great to have an in at the station. "What's someone like Tiffany doing working at a police station? She's not a police officer, is she?" Max couldn't picture Tiffany, with her blue hair and black eyeliner in a uniform.

Eric laughed. "No, she's doing clerical work. It's just temporary. She got accepted to grad school, but it doesn't start until August."

Then Max's smile faded. "It would be wrong to ask her for information."

"You could look at it that way, but what I think would be wrong is someone getting away with murder. Someone who would strangle a woman on the beach is someone who could kill again. They need to be behind bars for the rest of their lives."

"You have a point there. By the way, how did you find out that Tiffany is working at the police station?"

"Her husband sent flowers to her at work. Those two are just adorable— I mean they're really cute. You know, like two puppies. Not like stray kittens at all."

"You're making fun of me. I hate it when you do that."

"I can't help myself, Max. You're just so—"

"If you call me adorable…"

"I was about to say you're so easy to tease. And you're such a good sport. It's one of the things I love about you. I don't have to watch what I say around you. Do you know how important that is in a friend? And rare?"

Max sighed. She didn't want him to walk on eggshells around her. She had been a bit testy lately. Maybe it was just Gabby's death that was putting her on edge. "Of course you can say anything to me. You know that." She sighed. "Just don't call me adorable."

"Who's adorable?" Jonathan asked, sliding into a barstool next to Eric.

"No one," Max said. "Except maybe you two."

"Aw, you're sweet, Max," Jonathan said. "You always say the nicest things. I wonder if you could teach Eric how to be a bit more, um…"

"Diplomatic?" Max suggested.

"Hey," Eric said, "if you're going to talk about me, do it behind my back like normal people."

Jonathan laughed. "You got it. Enough about you. I want to hear about the dead body Max found. What's up with that?"

"I didn't find Gabby's body. Olivia did. I just came running when she started screaming."

"How gruesome," Jonathan said, shaking his head. "What does this make? Three? What's happened to our lovely little town? Is it even safe to be out and about with a murderer on the loose? Maybe we should move somewhere with a lower crime rate, like Detroit. What do you think, Eric?"

"Very funny," Eric said in a voice that indicated he was not amused. "None of the murders were connected. It's just a fluke. It could happen anywhere."

"If you say so," Jonathan said. "Let's talk about something more cheerful, shall we? How's the bridal business?"

After a sufficient amount of small talk, Eric and Jonathan left her to be seated in the dining room. The crowd at the bar had thinned out, but it would get busy again when the band started playing at nine. Burt came over to her and asked her if she wanted another glass of wine. She was thinking over the question when he went ahead and refilled her glass.

"It's on me," he said. "You don't have to finish it. You're walking, right?"

"As usual," she said. "I'm pretty sure I'm going to finish it. It's been a rough few days."

"That's one way to put it,' he said as he wiped off wine glasses absentmindedly. "I heard you found the dead woman's body. That must have been a shock."

"You can say that again. Olivia found her but I got there right after. Gabby was Olivia's friend, so it was the biggest shock for her. She's really shaken up about it."

"It's all everyone's been talking about," Burt said. "I heard someone surprised her on the beach and strangled her. Was it robbery?"

"It doesn't seem that way." Apparently, Burt hadn't heard anything relevant or useful. At that moment, she didn't want to talk about murder anymore.

"Max?" She heard a voice behind her and turned around to see Quinn and Ashley.

"Hi!" Max said. "What are you doing here?" Then realizing that might sound rude, added, "Want to join me? They have a really good bar menu."

Ashley appeared distracted as she looked around the restaurant, but Quinn said, "Sure, we'd love to," and pulled up a barstool next to her. Ashley sat on the other side of Quinn.

"Where's Nicholas?" Max looked around but didn't see him.

"He's at home eating leftover pizza," Quinn said. "He wasn't feeling sociable. We were getting cabin fever and needed to get out. This place has great reviews."

"Nicholas would be a recluse if it weren't for you," Ashley said. "He's lucky to have you."

"It's not like that really. We're both homebodies so were a good match." Quinn ordered a pomegranate martini from Burt, and Ashley opted for a glass of Merlot.

Max searched her mind for appropriate topics of conversation. She really wanted to find out who had a prescription for Zolpidem. She'd have to be crafty to learn anything.

"So, how did you and Nicholas meet?" she asked Quinn. "Olivia said you didn't know each other in college."

"It's ironic that we went to the same school for three years and only met after we both graduated, isn't it?" Quinn took a sip of her drink. "Actually, Ashley met him first. Olivia never told you the story?"

"No," Max lied, hoping to hear Quinn's version of events. She looked over at Ashley who had already downed half her glass of wine.

"Well, you know Ashley is a nurse, don't you? She specializes in pain management, and Nicholas was in a lot of pain while he was healing from his fractured ankle. They had to do two surgeries and he was in and out of the hospital for weeks. He asked her out, but Ashley, ever the professional, said she couldn't date a patient."

"But we did get to be friends," Ashley said. "And one day I had him over to the house for dinner. He took one look at Quinn and that was it."

"Really? So it was love at first sight," Max said.

"It was for Nicholas," Ashley said. "He had to convince Quinn, but in the end he won her over. Quinn's not one to jump into anything."

"I'm just more practical," Quinn said. "It's good that one of us is."

"So Nicholas isn't practical?" Max asked.

"Let's just say I'm the one who makes sure the bills are paid. Nicholas just goes with the flow. It keeps things interesting."

"Right now I wish life were a bit less interesting," Ashley said.

Max saw her opening. "I know what you mean," Max said. "I've been having trouble sleeping since the murder."

"Me, too," Quinn agreed. "I lie down and can't stop thinking about Gabby."

"Yes, it must be even worse for you, since you knew her. I'd only met her that day." Max took a sip of her wine and tried to be nonchalant when she asked, "Have you ever taken anything to help you sleep? I was thinking of asking my doctor for a prescription."

Ashley glared at her. Was that her answer? "Who told you?"

"Who told me what?" Max tried to sound innocent.

"Don't give me that," Ashley snapped. Her barstool scraped loudly as she stood up and pushed it aside. She lowered her voice as if she didn't want anyone else to hear. "Someone told you that they found sleeping pills in her system and that I had the prescription." Burt stopped wiping a glass and looked in their direction.

"No one told me that," Max said, leaving out the part about how she knew what was in the coroner's report.

"Did you give her sleeping pills?"

"No, I didn't." Ashley leaned over Quinn and pointed a finger at Max. "And you better not be spreading lies about me," she hissed. She stormed out of the bar and out the front door of the restaurant.

Quinn called Burt over, but Max told her she'd take care of the bill so she could chase after Ashley. She felt responsible for upsetting her, but she was also pleased that she'd learned a very important piece of information. Still, the most important piece was missing. Why would Ashley give Gabby sleeping pills? And did Gabby take them voluntarily, or had Ashley somehow slipped them to her?

Max paid the bill and stepped out of the front door of the Quick Fox and into the cool night. She hugged her sweater close to her and waited for an opening in the traffic so she could cross Coast Highway. A block north she turned up Rose Street toward her home. The street was empty, which wasn't unusual at this time of night, but it didn't normally make her uneasy the way it did tonight. Shadows stretched across the sidewalk and her heels echoed in the silence.

She was relieved when she saw her dad's lights on, but was surprised he was home so early from his date. She thought about stopping in to see him, but she knew he would scold her for walking home alone. She'd done it countless times before, but things were different now with a murderer on the loose.

She walked up the steps to her apartment. She'd feel better when she was inside with a nice cup of tea. As she was unlocking her door, she looked at the glass panes in her door. Someone could break one of them and unlock the door from outside. She shivered as she stepped inside, locking the deadbolt. Maybe a security screen door was not such a bad idea. There was a lock on her bedroom door, and tonight she would be using it. Someone needed to solve this murder so they could all go back to feeling safe.

Chapter Twenty-Two

Max almost didn't go to the beach Wednesday morning. She wanted Jason to be happy, she just didn't want to see him being happy with another woman who wasn't her. But she needed to talk with him, so she put on her cutest workout clothes and pulled her hair into a perky ponytail and headed down the street toward the ocean.

She looked up and down the coast but didn't see him. Her mood matched the gray skies and she plopped down on the sand sitting cross-legged and watching the waves crash against the shore.

The air was cool for late June, and she shivered. She jumped when Detective Cruz sat down next to her.

"You need to make more noise when you're sneaking up on someone," she snapped.

"Sorry," he said. "Would you like me to leave?"

"No. I'm sorry. I'm just on edge. And while I'm apologizing, I'm also sorry I got mad at you the other day. I know you were just doing your job."

"You're not just apologizing so I'll share information, are you?"

She turned to look at him, about to snap at him again, when she saw the smile on his face and the twinkle in his eye. Why did everyone love teasing her? "That's not the reason, but if you were willing to tell me anything useful, I would be willing to listen."

"There's not much to tell, really," he admitted.

Max knew if he did have information he had no problem telling her to stay out of police business. Although there was the little detail about the sleeping pills. She couldn't bring it up without putting Keiko at risk. She didn't know what the police would do to Keiko if they found out she'd hacked into the coroner's computers.

"What about the guy from the sketch. Did you find him?"

"Yes. And you just happened to see him on Zinnia Street?" He sounded skeptical.

"Well…" She really hated lying to him.

"Max? Tell me the truth."

"Okay," she said with a sigh. "I saw him on the beach and followed him. I was keeping plenty of distance. At least I thought I was. I just wanted to see where he was going so I could tell you."

His eyes narrowed and his face reddened. "How could you do something so stupid?" he asked.

"I know it was stupid. I just wasn't thinking. I didn't want him to get away without finding out where he was going. So did you find out where he lives?"

"We found him at a halfway house. But he has an alibi for the night of the murder, so you risked your neck for nothing. Promise me you won't do anything like that again."

"I promise," she said sheepishly, disappointed that the stranger wasn't the murderer. "It has to be one of Olivia's friends."

"You think so?" Cruz sounded noncommittal, still scowling at her.

"I thought you liked bouncing ideas off me. What's changed?"

Jason stared out at the ocean and for a moment Max wondered if he were going to answer the question. He sighed deeply. "This case has me worried. You're too close to the suspects. I don't like it. And then you go following random people who could be dangerous."

"I was pretty darn close to the suspects before, but you didn't shut me down like you are this time."

Jason gave her a sideways glance. "I was okay as long as I didn't realize how much danger you were in. I want to keep you safe."

"Well, don't you think I'd be safer if I knew what was going on? I know better than to be alone with any of them, but what if they were all in on it together?" At that moment, she realized that was a possibility. "What if they were all in on it? Do you think that's possible?"

"All I know is I've got several suspects and no motive. There seems to be no reason for Nicholas, Quinn, or Ashley to want her dead. And I can't come up with a reason for a stranger to kill her."

"Nicholas is hiding something," Max said. "I told you about the conversation he had with Gabby that night. She threatened to tell Quinn something. Maybe he killed her to keep her quiet."

"That's one idea," Jason agreed. "But it would help if we knew what he was hiding."

Max had given this question a lot of thought since the night of the murder. "Maybe it had to do with the fire that killed his family. Keiko found some old newspaper articles, and it looks like the fire may have been suspicious."

"You think Nicholas had something to do with it?" Jason asked.

"Maybe. What if he set the fire and Gabby somehow knew? That would be one reason to want to keep her quiet. What's the statute of limitations on arson?" she asked.

"It varies depending on the jurisdiction and other factors. I'll call the San Francisco PD and see what I can find out." He rose and smiled down at her. "You're right. It does help to talk it over with you. Sorry I was shutting you out. I just don't want to see you get hurt."

Max stood up and brushed the sand off her pants. "I don't want to see me get hurt either. Will you let me know what you find out about the fire?"

"Will do." He reached out his hand. "Friends again?"

Max hesitated. "Of course." She took his hand and felt a tingle move from her hand to the rest of her body. Why did he always have that effect on her?

oOo

Max expected to have coffee and oatmeal by herself, since her dad went to yoga class on Wednesday morning, but when she came through the back door into his kitchen she found him sitting at the dining room table. He looked a bit forlorn.

"No yoga this morning?" she asked, wondering what had him out of sorts. She poured a cup of coffee and sat down across from him.

Richard gave her a sheepish look. "I can't go to yoga class anymore," he admitted.

"Why not?"

"I'd rather not talk about it," he said, getting up to refill his cup.

Max was perplexed. Why would her dad not be able to go to yoga class? "Does this have anything to do with you being home so early from your date? Did you tick someone off?" That was not like him.

"Sort of," he said. Then, he seemed to realize his daughter wasn't going to give up until he told her what had happened. "I took one of the women to dinner a week or so ago. It was just a friendly dinner, no big deal."

"Uh-huh," Max said, waiting for the rest of the story.

"Then Irena invited me over for a home cooked meal. She's a really good cook."

"I see. So, Irena found out about the other woman?" Max tried hard not to snicker.

Her dad frowned. "She made a big deal out of it. I never implied that I was interested in anything serious with either of them," he protested. "Now I have to avoid both of them. And I liked that yoga class."

Max laughed. He gave her a pained look at first, and then started to smile. Max leaned over and gave him a kiss on the cheek. "My dad, the lady killer. This is a whole new side of you I haven't seen before," she teased. He gave her a look that said he wasn't amused. "So you're just going to avoid the whole situation? That doesn't sound like you. It's certainly not how you taught me to deal with things."

"It's just..." he began, then sighed. "You're right. So what should I do?"

Giving her dad dating advice was something new for her. "Call each of them up and talk to them. Explain that you are not ready for anything serious. I'm sure they'll understand."

He seemed to brighten up. "You think so? It would be nice to go back to yoga class."

"I have an idea," she said. "Why don't you see if you can get a group to go out for coffee afterwards? It would be good for you to be out with people more. But in the future, if you ask someone out, let them know up front if you just want to be friends. It's safer that way."

"Thanks, sweetie. That's very good advice. I used to be able to have women friends, since everyone knew I was happily married. I miss that. I'm not in any rush to get involved in a relationship."

"Good. There's no reason for you to rush into anything." Her dad would find the right person eventually. Not someone to replace her mom, but a person to start a new chapter of his life with. And she'd find someone, too.

She put her cup in the dishwasher, said her goodbyes and headed up the street for her morning walk to work.

Max called Olivia to check on her and was told she and Zach were taking Quinn, Nicholas, and Ashley on the train to San Juan Capistrano for the day. San Juan Capistrano was best known for its historic mission, but it also had charming shops, plenty of great places to eat, and a beautiful beach. Max was a little disappointed she wasn't going. Did Olivia not invite her because Ashley was mad at her? Or did she just assume Max couldn't go because she had her shop to run?

The first thing Max did after turning the open sign around was to call Tiffany. Would she know anything from working at the police station? There was only one way to find out. They made arrangements to meet for lunch at Rose Street Café at noon. Tiffany didn't ask why Max wanted to meet with her, but Tiffany was no dummy, so she probably knew the reason. Max hoped she didn't mind being pumped for information, and she especially hoped that Tiffany had information that she was willing to share.

Keiko came into work early again, wearing a red mini dress with a white Peter Pan collar and a flower in her hair. After a quick hello, she went straight to the office and got to work updating their website with pictures of the latest gowns that had just arrived. When Keiko had her mind on a task, there was little that could distract her.

Max looked over Keiko's shoulder while she worked, giving her input, but her mind was not on the gowns. "I don't really like Olivia hanging out with three murder suspects, but it's not like I can tell her to stay away from them. She refuses to believe that any of them had anything to do with Gabby's murder."

"That is understandable," Keiko said. "They are her friends, after all."

Max realized she was only keeping Keiko from doing her job, and it would be better if she got out of her hair. "I'm going to go upstairs and start steaming the new dresses."

"I can do that when I get done here," Keiko said, helpful as always.

"Thanks, but I need something to keep me busy. The only appointment we have today is Lori's. I don't suppose you've thought of a way to get me out of it?" Her face lit up. "I know, I could say we've gone out of business."

Keiko stopped what she was doing and turned around in her chair to face Max. "You'll get through it. I'll be here to help."

Max sighed. "We're not exactly in a position to turn business away, so I guess I don't have a choice."

"You make it sound like you're on the verge of going bankrupt. We have three appointments tomorrow and four on Friday, so there is nothing for you to concern yourself about. We are just as busy since you took over the shop as we were when Darlene owned it."

"I'm afraid I'm a worrier. I don't know what it will take me to be convinced that the shop is successful."

"You're such a worrier, you worry about worrying." Keiko shook her head and the huge red flower in her hair wobbled precariously. "But you have me to remind you that everything is great. I am like your Jiminy Cricket."

"I thought he was Pinocchio's conscience," Max said, wondering where Keiko was going with this, not for the first time.

"Jiminy Cricket is the small voice reminding you of what is right and wrong. And what is right is this shop and how well it is doing. And what is wrong is worrying over things you have no control over."

"I see. That is very wise of you." Max smiled, amused by Keiko's logic.

"Thank you." Keiko nodded in agreement. "Wisdom can come from many places."

"That sounds like something River might say."

"It is something he said. I think it's a quote," Keiko admitted.

Max laughed. "Why does that not surprise me? If you need me, I'll be upstairs."

"And if you need me," Keiko said, "I will be right here." She turned back around and got back to work on the website.

Max climbed the steps and pulled the steamer out of the corner and began steaming the newly arrived wedding gowns to get out the creases. She enjoyed the process, getting to know each dress as she worked, imagining the bride that would be perfect for a particular dress. After she finished with each one, she hung it up in the rack along the side of the room in order of style and color, from pure white to ecru. When she finished, she'd figure out which ones to take downstairs for the main display.

Max heard Keiko calling up to her and came down the steps. "What's up?"

"You have a text from Olivia. I thought it might be important."

Olivia's text said that Bob Karsten, Gabby's father, might be calling Max. Olivia apologized for giving him Max's number, but she wouldn't be home until late and Bob was only in town for one day.

As soon as she finished reading the text, the phone rang. It was Gabby's father. He had flown into town as soon as he heard about his daughter's death. Max wondered why it had taken until

Wednesday for him to arrive when Gabby had died on Saturday, but she didn't ask. After offering her condolences, Max invited him to come to the shop.

When Max heard the door jingle, she entered the showroom and found a short man with thinning hair and a rumpled suit. He squinted through wire-rimmed glasses.

"Are you Max?" the man asked.

"Mr. Karsten?" Max was expecting someone bigger and burlier, not someone who looked like an accountant.

"Call me Bob, please."

Max offered him a cup of tea, wishing there were more she could do for the grieving father.

"I only found out yesterday," he said. "The police had trouble locating me. Her mother was still listed as her emergency contact even though she passed away years ago. They told me how she died."

"I'm so sorry," Max said. "It must be a terrible shock."

"I had hoped she would turn her life around. I kept on hoping no matter how many times she let me down. I was always afraid I'd get a phone call telling me she was gone, but I never expected this. Her mother hardly let me see her when she was a child, and once she grew up she didn't want much to do with me until after her mother died. I finally got to know my only daughter." He shook his head and wiped a tear away. "I'm sorry to burden you with this. I gather you barely knew Gabrielle."

"I just met her on Saturday." She offered him a tissue, but he waved the box away. "She seemed so full of life."

"I want to see her body. I need to, just to believe it's really true. I called Olivia to see if she would take me to the morgue.

Olivia was always such a good friend to Gabrielle, I was hoping she'd do me that favor. They're expecting me at the morgue at eleven, so I'd better get going. I have a flight home tonight."

"I'll go with you," Max said impulsively.

Bob looked up, a mixture of surprise and hope on his face, and Max knew it was the right thing to do.

"You don't need to do that for me," he said.

"Yes, I do. Do you have a car?"

"I have a rental."

"Let's go." Max stood up and grabbed her purse.

Max let Keiko knew she would be out for a while and she and Bob got in his car and headed toward Coast Memorial Hospital.

oOo

When Bob dropped Max off and headed for the airport, Max plopped down on one of the chairs in the showroom.

"Would you like some tea?" Keiko asked. "I don't have anything stronger than that to offer you."

Max smiled. "Thanks. That would be lovely."

Keiko brought Max a cup of rose tea with one sugar, just the way she liked it. "How did it go?" Keiko asked with concern in her voice.

"I waited in another room while Bob went to see Gabby. I can't imagine how difficult this must be for him. He's racked with guilt, thinking he could have been a better father, and now he won't have the chance to fix things."

"It was a kind thing you did to go along with him."

"Sometimes, you just know what the right thing to do is. Then it's an easy decision to make. It's those times when you can't tell what the right thing is that are hard. And that's most of the time. At least for me."

"I know what you mean," Keiko agreed. "Life is rarely black and white. By the way, did you ask if he knew who might have killed her?"

"Well, not in those words. I did ask if there was anyone he knew of who might have wanted to do her harm."

"And?" Keiko prodded impatiently.

"He didn't know much about her life or her friends. Or enemies for that matter."

Max took another sip of tea, feeling revived. "I think I'll steam some more dresses. That always cheers me up."

"If you say so," Keiko said skeptically. "I will go to work downloading the rest of the pictures for the new dresses so I can add them to the website."

"Good idea," Max said. "What would I do without you?"

"You would find someone else who is not as talented as me and miss me terribly." She made a face and turned to go back into the office.

"That is so true." Max hoped she never had to find out.

CHAPTER TWENTY-THREE

Max rushed across the street hoping that she wouldn't be too late for her lunch date with Tiffany. She walked through the doors of the café and looked around for a woman with blue hair. Tiffany waved at her from a corner table, but her hair was no longer blue. It was pink.

"Your hair looks great!" Max said. "Although I really liked the blue."

"Me, too." Tiffany stood and gave her a hug. "I'm thinking of going back to it. But I felt the need for a change and it was cheaper and less painful than another tattoo."

"I'm buying," Max insisted. "What would you like? They have really good veggie burgers, if you like that sort of thing. I'm getting an avocado sandwich. It's my favorite."

"Veggie burger sounds great," Tiffany said.

After putting in their orders at the counter, Max returned to the table, handing Tiffany her lemonade and sitting down with her iced tea.

"How's married life?" she asked.

Tiffany grinned. "It's wonderful. We're talking about starting a family. We probably should wait until I finish with grad school, but I'm not sure if we want to wait that long."

"That's awesome," Max said sincerely. "You'll make a great mom."

184

"Okay, that's enough small talk," Tiffany said with a grin. "I know why you really invited me to lunch."

"You do?" Max tried to sound innocent, but wasn't sure she succeeded.

Tiffany took a sip of her lemonade and looked Max in the eye. "I can't give you any information about the murder investigation. It would be against policy. Plus if Detective Cruz found out he'd have my head."

Max's eyes widened. "Would he fire you?"

Tiffany laughed. "He can't fire me, but he could probably get me written up."

"Well, I wouldn't want that," Max said. This lunch was turning out to be a disappointment.

"It's just a temporary job. But they do trust me, and I wouldn't want to disappoint them."

The waiter put a veggie burger down in front of Tiffany and a sandwich in front of Max.

"Well, I'm glad we got together anyway. I haven't seen you since the wedding." Max took a big bite of her sandwich. "Keiko showed me pictures. You looked stunning."

"Thanks to Keiko." Tiffany said. "And you, of course."

"It was a gorgeous gown, but Keiko gets most of the credit. She's pretty amazing."

Tiffany looked around as if checking to see if anyone was listening. "She's really good with research too, isn't she?"

"Mmm hmm," Max murmured with her mouth full. She hoped Tiffany didn't know anything about Keiko trying to hack into the police database.

"So," Tiffany said, leaning closer. "I'm sure she's looked at Gabrielle's social media accounts and checked out her online friends."

This was more like it. "I'm sure she has, but she hasn't mentioned anything about it."

"She didn't mention that Gabby had an online friend who lives in Crystal Shores?"

Max's ears perked up. "Not that I recall. I'll have to ask her about it."

"Yes," Tiffany said with a smile. "Do that."

oOo

When Max got back to the shop, she gave Keiko the information that Tiffany had divulged. Sure enough, Keiko had been through Gabby's online profiles, but she hadn't noticed anything out of the ordinary.

"I copied a list of all her online friends," Keiko said, opening up her laptop. "I didn't know how long before her accounts would be shut down. Besides, if someone wanted to hide something, they would unfriend her right away. I'm hoping they didn't do it before I was able to make the list. I didn't recognize any of the names, but maybe you will. Here." Keiko turned the laptop toward Max. "Take a look. Do you recognize anyone?"

Max peered at the computer screen and then gasped. "Burt Norgrove!"

"You know him?" Keiko asked.

"He's the bartender at the Quick Fox. How did he get to be online friends with Gabby?"

"Maybe Gabby met him when she visited Olivia before," Keiko suggested. "I mean, he does work at a bar and she does like to drink."

Max scrunched up her face while she pondered this. It was possible, but if that was the case, Olivia should know about it, shouldn't she?

Max dialed Olivia who picked up on the first ring. She got right to the point. "Did you know Gabby was friends with Burt?"

"Burt the bartender?" Olivia asked. "I don't think she ever met him."

"He's her friend online."

"Really. Well, that's odd. Although the Quick Fox is walking distance from my place, so I suppose she could have gone there when she went on one of her so-called walks. But why would they have stayed in touch?"

"I don't know, but I'm going to see if I can find out."

Olivia invited Max and Keiko to dinner that evening since her parents had just arrived in town. Quinn, Ashley, and Nicholas would also be joining them. Max accepted but Keiko had plans.

"I'll see you tonight, then," Max told Olivia. "I'll let you know if I learn anything."

oOo

All thoughts of Burt left Max's mind when Lori arrived at four o'clock sharp. She didn't appear like her usual confident self. She was impeccably dressed as always, but her hair hung limply and there were circles under her eyes.

Max introduced her to Keiko, and invited Lori to have a seat. "Have you brought some pictures for me of dresses you like?"

"No," Lori said quietly. "I was hoping we could talk." She sounded serious and not particularly happy.

Keiko took that as her cue to disappear. "I will be in the office if you need me," she said, leaving Max to deal with Lori on her own.

Max sat across from her and asked, "Is everything okay?"

"I'm not sure," Lori said, flipping her blond hair over one shoulder. "I told Jason I stopped by to see you and he didn't seem happy about it." She slumped back in the chair. "He's been snapping at me, which is just not like him. I don't know what's up with him lately."

"He does have a murder to solve," Max suggested.

"True. But I thought he'd be excited about the idea of getting married, even if he isn't ready to propose. We have a great relationship. We have so much in common. We both work in law enforcement and we like to do so many of the same things."

Max hoped Lori wasn't going to tell her about their sex life. She might have to cover her ears and go "lalalalala," until Lori stopped.

"You work in law enforcement?" Max asked.

"I work for the D.A.'s office," Lori said. "I'm an attorney. Didn't Jason ever talk about me? We've been going out for seven months."

"Well," Max said, "I don't see that much of Detective-- I mean Jason. We just see each other in passing from time to time."

"Oh, I see. For some reason, I thought you two were close."

Did Max imagine that Lori looked suspicious when she said this? "I guess you could say we worked together on a couple of cases. When he's focused on a case you can hardly talk to him about anything else. Sometimes I crack jokes just to get a smile out of him, but it rarely works."

"I do that, too!" Lori said. "He just looks at me like I'm being annoying."

"I know that look," Max said. She was starting to feel sympathy toward her rival. It wasn't her fault she was beautiful, intelligent, and successful, after all.

"What is it about you that makes you so easy to talk to?" Lori asked.

Max shrugged. "Maybe all those years of listening to brides?"

"Maybe," Lori said, "but I think it's your eyes."

"My eyes?"

"Yes." Lori leaned back in her chair. "You have kind eyes. It's like someone with such kind eyes wouldn't judge me for what I have to say."

Max felt a twinge of guilt. She was plenty judgmental. It was one of the things she wanted to improve about herself. She was lucky other people weren't aware of it.

"Thank you," Max finally said. "That's very nice of you to say."

"Maybe we should go to lunch sometime," Lori suggested.

No, no, no! Lori was the last person she wanted to go to lunch with. She needed an excuse, and quick. "I don't usually go to lunch during the week. I'm too busy with the shop."

"Maybe drinks some time then," Lori said, standing up. "I won't take up any more of your time. I guess I'll see you at Olivia's wedding."

"The wedding's cancelled," Max said just as Lori got to the door.

"Oh, that's too bad." Lori turned around, one hand on the doorknob. "Is it because of the murder?"

"Yes, Olivia didn't feel right about getting married on the beach not far from where her friend died, and she couldn't find another venue on such short notice."

"I guess I'll see you around then," Lori said.

After Lori left, Max was more confused than ever. Jason could do a lot worse than Lori, but did he want to marry her? Max didn't know if he even wanted to get married at all. Maybe he was a confirmed bachelor. No, Max didn't believe that for a second. Something told her that Jason was the settling down kind. She knew for sure that he wasn't one to jump into anything and forget talking him into doing something that wasn't his own idea. If he were going to marry Lori or anyone, it would be his idea.

The door jingled and Max looked up to see a familiar face. "Curtis!" She ran over to give him a hug. Max and Keiko used to see Curtis almost daily when he worked as a deliveryman before he got a job he liked better up in Los Angeles. He had a huge crush on Keiko, and Max had a feeling that might be why he was there. "How have you been? Are you still working at that video game company?"

"Yes, after I finished my internship, they offered me a permanent job. It's an amazing place to work. Next time you're in L.A, you should stop by the campus for a tour."

"That would be great. I'm sure Keiko would love it, too," Max said.

Curtis smiled. "I've already shown her around the place. We had lunch together at the commissary. I'm surprised she didn't tell you about it. I still pinch myself that I get to work there. There's a game room where we can play video games any time we want and a really cool pirate themed coffee shop where everything is free. My first day I drank so many cappuccinos I couldn't get to sleep that night."

"That sounds amazing," Max said. "Not the part about not being able to sleep, but the rest of it."

"Yeah, I limit myself to two cups of coffee these days," he said with a grin.

Keiko came out from the office. "Curtis. What are you doing here?"

Max had tried to teach Keiko to be more diplomatic, but it hadn't helped. She always said just what she meant.

"I got off work early and I couldn't wait to see you," he said. He took one step toward her and she took one step back.

Max looked at the two young people. Keiko was blushing.

"Are you two...?" Max asked.

"Yes," Curtis said at the same time Keiko said, "We're just friends."

"I see," said Max, grinning. "If you say so." She wanted to ask Keiko if that were the case then why was she blushing, but she held her tongue.

"Okay, friend," Curtis said. "Do you think your boss will let you get off work a little early? My family will be at the Beachcomber at six. They can't wait to meet you."

"You can take off now if you want, Keiko," Max said, enjoying seeing how uncomfortable Keiko was. She was a very private person and normally Max wouldn't intrude, but she felt partially responsible for getting the two of them together and that made her very happy. She knew how much Curtis adored Keiko.

"Fine," Keiko said and went to gather her things. When she returned, she said to Max, "I guess it's time you knew. I just hate it when you're right."

oOo

Dinner at Chez Mer wasn't until seven, which gave Max enough time to stop at the Quick Fox first.

She stepped inside the dimly lit lobby of the restaurant and headed straight for the bar. The lounge area was nearly empty. Burt looked up from polishing glassware and smiled.

"Hi Max," he said. "What'll it be?"

Max pulled out a barstool and sat down. "Information."

Burt raised his eyebrows but said nothing.

She leaned forward on the bar and spoke quietly. "I know you were friends with Gabby. Why didn't you tell me?"

"What makes you think we were friends?" Burt asked evasively.

What was he hiding? Burt took a cloth and began wiping down the bar, even though it looked as if it had been freshly polished. Max glanced at a couple at the end of the bar who averted their eyes.

"Why are those people staring at me?" Max felt suddenly uncomfortable in her friendly neighborhood bar.

Burt looked over his shoulder at them and then back to Max. "I expect it's because you keep finding dead bodies."

"I do not," Max said, indignantly. She just happened to be around when they turned up. It was hardly her fault. "You're Gabby's friend online. It's there for anyone to see. I'm sure the police have questioned you. Why won't you tell me? I'm trying to clear Olivia's name." And she was trying to catch a killer.

Burt stopped wiping and looked her straight in the eye. "Some things are private," he said.

"But she's dead," Max whispered. "I think she'd rather have her killer brought to justice rather than have you keep her secrets."

Burt put his elbows on the bar and leaned forward, also keeping his voice at a whisper. "It's called anonymous for a reason."

"Well, if you wanted to be anonymous, maybe you shouldn't have been her online friend."

"Yes, that was a mistake," he admitted. "The police found me that way, too. I've already told them everything."

Max thought back to all the times customers had offered to buy him drinks and he always said he didn't drink on the job. Had he given up drinking completely? "Were you her sponsor?"

"Not exactly," he said. "Just someone she could reach out to when she was here. I met her at a meeting the last time she was visiting Olivia, and I gave her my number and email in case she needed to talk to someone. She used to email me all the time. I think she liked having someone who was an outsider that she could talk to, someone who didn't judge her. She called me that night."

"She did?" He had her attention now. "What did she say?"

"I didn't answer. I never do when I'm working, but I wish I had that one time. I listened to the message later, and I could tell she'd been drinking. She sounded happy, but then drunks always do. Either happy or angry. I get both kinds here pretty much every night. I like the happy ones better."

"What exactly did she say?"

Burt paused as if he didn't want to tell her more, but then gave in. "She said she could pay back the money I loaned her."

"You loaned her money?" It came out a little too loud and the people at the end of the bar looked over again. More quietly, she asked, "Why?"

"So she could come here for the wedding. She was broke and miserable that she wouldn't be able to see Olivia get married. I bought her a plane ticket." He added sadly, "Now I wish I hadn't."

"You had no way of knowing what would happen. That was very kind of you." She always knew Burt had a soft spot. "But if she was broke, where was she getting the money to pay you back?"

"She didn't say. I thought maybe Olivia was giving it to her. Gabby said she didn't want to ask her but maybe she changed her mind."

"Maybe," Max said. She'd have to ask Olivia when she got the chance.

oOo

Since Chez Mer wasn't far, Max decided to walk up Coast Highway to the restaurant. She peered in the windows of the shops as she walked past furniture stores and clothing boutiques. Few stores stayed open evenings in their sleepy little town.

Once she arrived, Olivia insisted that she sit between her and her mother whom Max had only met once before. Zach sat next to Olivia, and Olivia's friends sat across the table.

Mrs. Cavendish leaned over to speak to Max. "Thank you for being there for Olivia through all this. She's lucky to have you as a friend."

"I'm the lucky one," Max said truthfully. "Your daughter is pretty darn special."

"We think so." Olivia's mother reached over and squeezed her husband's hand.

"What's that?" He smiled at his wife. "What do we think?"

"Never mind, dear."

Max smiled at the affection the couple showed for each other after more than thirty years of marriage. It reminded her of her parents who had playfully teased each other but never went too far. She wanted a marriage like that some day.

The wine flowed freely, and Max noticed Nicholas refilled his glass several times. As their dinner plates were cleared away, he stood up and made a toast. "To the happy couple," he slurred. "No reason for a murder to put a damper on your big day."

"Sit down," Quinn hissed and tugged at his sleeve. Nicholas looked confused, but did as he was told.

"I'm sorry, everyone," Quinn said.

195

"What?" Nicholas asked, seemingly unaware that he was making everyone uncomfortable.

"It's okay," Olivia said. "I know this has been hard on everyone. Zach and I had a long talk and we decided to postpone the wedding."

"Good," Nicholas mumbled. "We can go home now."

"That detective told us not to leave town," Ashley said.

"I'll call him in the morning," Quinn said. "I don't think he can force us to stay if we want to go. After all, we've already told him everything we know."

Max frowned. She didn't want Olivia's friends leaving before the murder had been solved. She needed more time to investigate, and once they were back in San Francisco, how was she supposed to figure out if one of them killed Gabby?

Olivia's mother patted her on the shoulder. "Don't look so sad, Max. It's just a postponement." She gave her daughter a concerned look. "Right?"

Olivia reassured her that she and Zach were still getting married. "We'll probably have a small ceremony later in the year."

"And not on the beach," Zach said, and Olivia agreed.

The conversation returned to more mundane subjects, but Max's mind was elsewhere. She couldn't shake the feeling that if Nicholas wasn't the murderer, then he was the key to solving who was. An odd feeling came over her—a feeling that she had the information she needed if she could only put the pieces together.

Olivia's father told Nicholas how much he enjoyed his trilogy. "I heard they're making a movie based on them," he said.

"Yes," Quinn answered for her husband. "The first one is coming out next year. Hopefully, they don't ruin it like they do with so many books."

"I got paid," Nicholas said morosely. "They can do whatever they want with them."

Quinn looked embarrassed and there was an awkward silence at the table until Olivia's mother spoke. "I'm glad at least I finally got to meet the three of you. Olivia's told me so much about all of you. I feel like I know you already."

Max wondered how well any of them knew Quinn, Ashley, or Nicholas.

Olivia got up to go to the ladies' room, and Max hurried after her. Max watched Olivia refreshing her lipstick, until her friend turned to her.

"What's up?" Olivia asked.

"Well, now that you mention it, I did have something I wanted to ask you."

Olivia raised her eyebrows. "I can always tell when you're up to something. What is it?"

Max scowled. Was she that transparent? "I was just wondering if you had offered Gabby money."

"Why would I offer her money?" Olivia asked. "She didn't tell me she needed any."

"She'd borrowed the money for her plane ticket and the night she was killed she told that person she could pay him back. I'm wondering where she was getting the money."

"Who'd she borrow from?"

"It's a long story," Max said, not wanting to betray Burt's confidence. "Let's go back out to the table. Everyone's going to be wondering what happened to us."

Max took her seat, more curious than before about who had agreed to give Gabby money. She was sure Ashley wouldn't have - she still seemed ticked off about the money she hadn't paid back years ago. She watched Nicholas as he refilled his wine glass. There was something about him that bothered her. She thought back to the picture on the back of his book. The picture was only six years old and yet he had changed so much.

oOo

When Max got home to her little apartment shortly after ten, she was surprised to see a white, heavy-duty, screen door had already been installed. When her dad got his mind set on something, he didn't mess around. She was relieved that it wasn't as ugly as she was expecting. Stepping inside and closing the screen door, she turned the deadbolt. A key lay on her dining room table with a note.

Just wanted to make sure my little girl is safe. Love, Dad.

Feeling safer than she had in days, Max fell asleep not more than a minute after she climbed into bed. She woke up the next morning before the alarm, and immediately her mind went to the fire that killed Nicholas's parents and brother. What had really happened? She had a feeling the answer to that question was the key to solving Gabby's murder.

As she lay in bed, all the pieces began to fit together and one thought came into perfect focus: Nicholas was not who he seemed to be. It was only a theory, but she was convinced she was right. How could she find out for sure? Quinn must know the truth about her husband. Or could he have kept the secret from her for all these years? She didn't know who she could trust.

Was the secret that Nicholas had kept for so long reason enough to kill?

She showered and dressed and tried to decide what to do next. A text arrived on her phone from Quinn.

Hi! It's Quinn. Olivia's stopping by for breakfast. Come, too.

Good. At least she'd have one more chance to question Quinn, Nicholas, and Ashley before they returned home.

Max borrowed her father's car and drove down Coast Highway. There was safety in numbers. As long as she wasn't alone with Nicholas, she'd be fine. But what if the others were in on it? She had no way of knowing if that was the case. At least Olivia would be there. Not that Olivia was going to protect them from a murderer. Maybe this was a bad idea. She called Detective Cruz and left him a message with her suspicions about Nicholas, making it as brief as possible, and let him know she was going to the beach house.

Quinn opened the door and looked surprised to see her.

"I got your text," Max said.

"What text?" Quinn asked.

Max showed her the text on her phone. Quinn said, "That's not my number." She stood there for a moment, then said, "You might as well come in. All we have is cereal, but you're welcome to join us."

Max followed Quinn to the kitchen, tossing the car keys on the countertop as she pulled up a stool at the breakfast bar. "Where's Nicholas and Ashley?" she asked.

"Nicholas went for a run and Ashley is sleeping in late."

"Good. I wanted to talk to you alone anyway," Max said. She paused. This would be an awkward conversation. "I wanted to ask about Nicholas. Or should I say Ian?"

Quinn laughed. "What are you talking about?"

"I think the fire killed Nicholas and your husband is really Nicholas's brother Ian," she blurted out.

Quinn narrowed her eyes. "How did you manage to jump to that conclusion?"

"Well, he shaved his head for one thing. Nicholas had dark brown hair and Ian's hair was lighter."

"That doesn't prove a thing," Quinn said.

"And he hasn't written anything since the fire," she added.

"He was traumatized," Quinn said sternly. "How dare you make an absurd accusation like that."

Max heard the sliding glass door from the veranda open and turned around to see Nicholas.

"Hi, Max. What's going on?" he asked. "You look upset, Quinn."

"Yes, I'm upset," Quinn snapped. "Max is making up ridiculous theories about you." She looked Max in the eye. "Next, I suppose you're going to say Nicholas murdered Gabby."

"No, of course not," Max said, glancing at Nicholas to see his reaction. She hoped Detective Cruz was on his way right now. It was reckless of her to question them without him. She had no one to protect her.

"Max said you're not Nicholas. You're actually Ian. I told her she's full of it."

Nicholas walked into the kitchen, got a glass out of the cupboard and poured himself some juice. Max waited nervously for him to finish drinking it. Finally, he put the empty glass down and spoke.

"It's true," he said, turning to Quinn. "I want you to know I had nothing to do with the fire. The police suspected arson at first, but they finally decided it was caused by some frayed electrical wires in the laundry room. I was sleeping in Nicholas's room. He wanted to stay up late writing, so he said he'd sleep on the sofa. I didn't have a room since my parents kicked me out of the house, but Nicholas talked them into letting me stay a few days while he was in town. Once the fire started I tried to go into my parents' room but their door was locked. I yelled to try and wake them up, but then the smoke got so thick I went back into the bedroom. I saw Nicholas's wallet, and for some reason I put it in my pocket. I guess for safekeeping. I could hardly breathe, so I finally climbed out of the window. I fractured my ankle in the fall and I was taken to the hospital. I was also treated for smoke inhalation."

"But didn't someone recognize you in the hospital?" Max asked, her curiosity getting the better of her. She looked over at Quinn to see how she was taking this news. Had she really never suspected?

"Nicholas was a virtual recluse. We had no other family, and he had no friends in San Francisco. I suppose he knew people in New York, but they never bothered to come see him. We looked a lot alike except for our hair color, so I shaved my head.

Nicholas had written me out of his will and left everything to his favorite charities. Our parents didn't have much money. The house he bought them was in his name. I got into some trouble when I was younger, but I was starting to be part of the family again when the fire happened. I had no money and no job. Everyone thought I was Nicholas, and it was just so easy to keep letting them think so. It wasn't that hard to avoid seeing people he knew until they just gave up and went away for good."

Max looked at Quinn, who was staring at Nicholas. Had she really never suspected all these years? "Why didn't you ever tell me?" she asked.

"It's hard keeping a secret that big, Quinn," he said. "I didn't want you to be burdened by it."

"And maybe you were afraid she'd leave you," Max said.

Nicholas hung his head. He spoke quietly. "I was sure of it. As Nicholas I could offer her a good life. As Ian, I could offer her nothing."

Ashley emerged from the bedroom in a tee shirt and yoga pants, her long hair messy.

"I have something to tell you," Nicholas said. "You may want to sit down."

"I heard everything. I figured it out years ago," she said. "I saw you in the hospital before you shaved your head, remember? It didn't take a genius to figure out that you were Ian, but I figured you weren't hurting anyone, so I played along. Besides, I've enjoyed the benefit of having a rich brother-in-law. I figured Max was getting too close to the truth, so I sent her a text to come over this morning to find out how much she knew."

"You sent the text?" Max was really confused now.

Ashley crossed her arms over her chest, looking determined. "If you've figured this much out, then you've probably figured out who killed Gabby, too. You brought your gun, Nicholas. You'll have to kill her, too."

Nicholas gasped. "What? I'm not killing anyone."

"You have a gun?" Max felt lightheaded.

"It's perfectly legal and I'm not planning to use it to kill anyone," Nicholas said. "I just feel safer having it with me."

Max stood frozen to the spot. She hoped Detective Cruz would burst through the door any moment, but she couldn't count on it. How was she going to get herself out of this one?

"I know you killed Gabby, Nicholas," Ashley said. "She was going to tell everyone your secret."

"I told her I would give her some money, and she agreed to keep quiet," Nicholas said. "It wouldn't have taken that much to buy her silence."

"I know you did it!" Ashley yelled at him. "I saw her body not long after you supposedly had your talk with her."

"She was fine when I went to see her." Nicholas looked from Ashley to Max. "Fine, but drunk. She fell asleep while I was talking to her so I left. She was very much alive when I left her." He turned back to Ashley. "You knew she was dead and you didn't tell anyone?"

"I knew it had to be you," Ashley said, grabbing his arm and shaking him. "Quinn was asleep and we know Olivia didn't kill her. Why won't you admit it? No one else had a reason to kill her but you. I thought the longer it took before anyone realized she was dead, the less likely they'd be able to prove it was you."

"You thought you were covering for me? I'm telling you I didn't do it," Nicholas insisted. "I don't know who did."

"Why are you lying to me?" Ashley slammed her hand down on the countertop angrily.

"He's not," Quinn coolly said. Her eyes were narrow slits as she stared at her husband. She turned to Max. "I'm the one who took care of Gabby. She was going to ruin everything. We're millionaires thanks to Nicholas. The real Nicholas, I mean, and his books. Why shouldn't we have the money? My husband was his brother. The money should have gone to him anyway. I'm not going back to living from paycheck to paycheck and living in a lousy apartment. I won't let anyone ruin it for us. I just need to take care of you and everything will be just the way it was." She snatched up Max's keys from the countertop, then turned and headed for her bedroom.

Nicholas's eyes were huge. "She knows where the gun is. You'd better run!"

"She took my keys!" Max didn't have time to think. She ran out onto the veranda, down the steps and kicked off her flip flops. She ran like she'd never run before, heading toward the boulders that separated Crystal Shores from Laguna Beach.

Leaping from boulder to boulder, she felt like she was eight years old again, with all the confidence of youth. She was halfway to the other side when she heard the first gunshot. She looked over her shoulder and saw Quinn fifty feet behind her with a gun pointed at her. She turned back in time to hear another bullet whiz by her head. As she ran, she told herself, "I can make it. I can make it."

Max heard a third gunshot and a cry. She hoped Quinn had fallen on the rocks, but she didn't turn around to make sure. She kept jumping across the rocks until she landed on the soft sand of Laguna Beach.

She ran past sunbathers and volleyball players and didn't slow down until she got to the street. She pulled her phone out of her pocket to call 9-1-1 when it rang. It was Detective Cruz. She panted, out of breath, and tried to get the words out.

"Quinn," she gasped. "Murderer."

"What are you talking about?" he asked.

She finally caught her breath and told him Quinn was the murderer, had a gun, and had tried to kill her. She figured the rest of the explanation could wait until later.

Chapter Twenty-Four

Saturday morning Max sat across from her dad sipping coffee. It seemed so normal, and she liked the way it felt. She hadn't walked on the beach since Quinn had tried to kill her. Someday she'd be able to see those boulders without the memory of running for her life. Or maybe not.

Her phone rang.

"Good morning, Zach," Max said. "What's up?"

"Good morning, Max," he answered. "I feel like getting married today."

"You do?" Max grinned. A wedding sounded like a great idea. Except for two things. She hadn't finished sewing her bridesmaid dress, and several women were expecting a sample sale today. Max took a deep breath. "That's great! At the gazebo?" The main beach had a large gazebo that was very popular for weddings.

"No. Olivia doesn't want to get married on the beach and I don't blame her. I found an even better place. There's no show at the theater this week, so we're going to do it there. They just finished the set for Hamlet. It will look like we're getting married on the steps of a castle."

"That's wonderful! How long have you been planning this?" She couldn't think of any news that would have made her happier this morning.

"Since Olivia said she wanted to cancel the wedding. I knew I was taking a chance, but I was hoping if she got up this morning and everything was taken care of, she'd go along with the plan. We're just inviting our family and close friends and we're keeping it casual, so tell your dad to put on his best Hawaiian shirt and get you there by seven. I hope your dress is ready to go."

Max ignored his last comment. "We'll be there."

After she hung up, Max thought about everything she needed to do. Then Olivia called and said to meet her at the salon at one. Apparently, Zach had not cancelled all the appointments he said he would.

"I can't make it to the salon," Max said and explained about the sample sale. She left out the part about not having finished her dress.

Olivia said Zach had only convinced her that morning to go through with the wedding and she couldn't wait to be his wife. Nicholas, or rather Ian, and Ashley had driven back to San Francisco after being held for questioning. They had abandoned Quinn. Max didn't judge them. She wasn't sure what she'd do if she found out one of her loved ones was a murderer. Ian would be penniless and would probably be sued by the charities that were supposed to benefit from Nicholas's will. He might even go to jail for fraud. Max almost felt sorry for him.

Max left the closed sign on the door. There would be no drop-ins today. The next several hours were a whirlwind getting ready for the invitation-only sale that would start at two o'clock. Keiko helped Max pull two portable clothes racks into the showroom and they hung the dresses she'd picked out on them.

Then she finished cutting out the fabric for her bridesmaid's dress.

Before she could start sewing, there was a knock on the back door and she panicked. She didn't have time for interruptions. Getting up from her sewing machine, she opened the door and saw Darlene standing there.

"I'm sorry," Max said apologetically. "I really don't have time to talk right now. Olivia's getting married this evening and I have tons to do."

Darlene ignored her protest and pushed past Max into the workroom. "What's going on?"

Max sighed. What part about not having time did her old boss not understand? "I'm having a small private sample sale, I have to finish my bridesmaid's dress, and I have to do my hair and makeup." Max heard the panic in her own voice. She was never going to get everything done in time.

"I just stopped by to say thank you. I'm going to be working with your father as a marketing consultant. In fact, I've decided to start a new consulting business. I haven't felt this alive since I sold the shop."

Darlene had a sparkle in her eye. "That's great," Max said, not wanting to be rude but feeling edgier by the moment. "But I've really got to finish this dress. Can we talk another time?"

"Let me take a look," Darlene said, picking up the pieces of fabric that needed to be a dress in a few hours. "I can finish this. Go take care of everything else."

Max stood for a moment not sure of what to do. "Thank you!" she finally gasped and rushed back into the showroom to finish getting ready for the brides who would appear soon.

The list of brides who needed dresses had swollen to ten and nine of them arrived early, no doubt to get the best selection. Max helped the women pick out dresses and Keiko took them back to the dressing room. Eight of the women chose dresses and Max took measurements for the alterations. One woman asked Max to hold a dress so she could bring in her mother to see it. The one holdout frowned and sulked as she looked at each dress Max showed her. She finally pulled a picture out of her purse.

"This was my dress. I want this dress. I'm sorry, but I just can't imagine getting married in anything else," she said sadly.

"When's your wedding?" Max asked.

"September. I don't want to postpone it, but I don't know what else to do. I've gone to two other bridal salons and they need at least four months to get it."

Max went upstairs and found the dress. She hated to sell a sample when she'd only had it a few months, but this was an emergency. She brought the dress downstairs and showed it to the bride. She burst into tears. Max hoped they were happy tears.

"I'm going to tell everyone about you," the bride said. "I have thousands of followers on social media and I am telling all of them about you and your store."

"Just don't tell them I can deliver a wedding dress in two months. This is a one-time only thing. Understand?"

After all the women had left, Max went back to the workroom just as Darlene sewed the last seam. All that was left was the hem.

"Go put it on and I'll mark the length for you," Darlene said.

Keiko pulled a curling iron out of her tote and after heating it up, joined Darlene and Max in the dressing room. Keiko curled Max's hair while she stood on the platform in the bridesmaid's dress and Darlene made chalk marks along the hem.

"Grab some scissors, Keiko," Max said, and when her assistant returned, she handed the scissors to Darlene. "I'm going to be late if I don't leave in five minutes. Just go ahead and cut it."

Keiko had her car keys in her hand ready to make a dash for the theater as soon as Darlene finished cutting the hem.

"I'll lock up," Darlene called after them as they ran out the front door. They jumped in Keiko's car and headed for the Crystal Shores Playhouse.

At seven o'clock, Max ran across the stage to Olivia, who stood next to Zach in front of the minister.

"You made it!" Olivia said, giving her friend a hug. "Barely."

"Sorry!" Max said, trying to catch her breath. "Crazy day. I'll tell you about it later." She looked out at the audience and saw Keiko sit down next to Richard. Then she recognized another person slipping into a seat and her heart did a familiar flip-flop.

She leaned close and whispered in Olivia's ear. "I thought you said just close friends and family. What's Detective Cruz doing here?"

"I've come to consider him a close friend. And when we're at my wedding, his name is Jason."

"Where's his date?" Max glanced out at the audience again, but Jason sat by himself in the third row.

Olivia only smiled and shrugged her shoulders.

The minister leaned over to Zach. "May we begin?"

"Yes!" Zach beamed.

Olivia and Zach had written their own vows. They faced each other, holding hands.

"Olivia," Zach began with a huge grin on his face. "I remember the first time I saw you. I thought you were the most beautiful woman I'd ever seen. I fell in love with you then, but that was before I knew what a big heart you have. I've fallen more and more in love with you each day. I've never met anyone so kind, caring and patient. You make me want to be the man who deserves you." He turned to the audience. "I could go on and on." Laughter filled the auditorium. "But don't worry. I won't." He turned back to Olivia. "I promise to love you and be there for you no matter what."

"Zachary," Olivia began, and Max could hear the smile in her voice even though she was standing behind her and couldn't see her face. "I tried to tell you I wasn't interested, but thank goodness you didn't listen to me. You seem to have a habit of not listening to me, but we'll talk about that later."

Zach laughed and Max heard chuckles coming from the audience.

Olivia continued. "You always make me smile, no matter what. I promise to be your partner in whatever adventures lay ahead for us. I will be there to wipe away your tears, whether they're from sadness, joy, or laughter. I realize now that everything can change in a moment." Now Olivia turned to the audience. "Tell your friends and family that you love them." She paused. "Right now," she said in a tone of voice that said she meant business. There were murmurs in the audience and Olivia turned around to face Max. "I love you," she said and Max saw

Olivia's eyes glistening with tears. Turning back to Zach, Olivia said, "I love you. I am yours forever."

By the time Olivia and Zach said "I do," there wasn't a dry eye to be found in the theater.

The wedding party and guests slowly moved into the lobby for the reception. By the time Max entered, she was disappointed to see a long line for champagne. She could use a drink after the day she'd had. Squeezing through the crowd saying hello to people she knew, she found her dad and filled him in about her hectic day at the shop.

"Hello, Max," Jason said from behind them. She turned around and smiled. Apparently, he'd gotten the memo, because he was wearing a Hawaiian shirt like most of the guests. He looked as handsome as ever.

Richard suddenly saw someone he needed to say hello to at just that moment and left them alone.

Jason handed her a glass of champagne.

"Thanks!" Max said gratefully and took a sip. "Where's Lori?" She looked over his shoulder for his girlfriend.

"She's not here," he said.

"Oh." Maybe something had come up and she couldn't make it. "It was a beautiful ceremony, wasn't it?"

"If you judge it on how many people cried, then it was exceptionally beautiful," he said, smiling.

"Did you cry?" she asked.

"Oh no," he said. "I'm a police detective. We don't cry."

Max looked at him skeptically. "Not even a little?"

"If I admit it, will you promise not to tell anyone ever? I have my reputation to protect."

"Sure." It was nice to talk to Jason without a murder hanging over their heads. She was glad Lori wasn't able to come, but then felt selfish thinking so. They stood together drinking their champagne as if neither of them knew what to say. "Is Lori okay?"

"Yeah, she's fine. She just—that is, we broke up," he said.

"Oh, that's too bad," Max said. She forced herself not to smile. Her heart started beating faster. Jason was single again.

"It is?" Jason said.

"What?"

"Too bad. You said it was too bad. I was hoping, well...."

"Why'd you break up?" she asked. "I mean, if you don't mind me asking."

"Turns out I had feelings for someone else. I finally admitted it to myself."

"Oh," Max said, her heart sinking. How many girlfriends did Jason have? She walked over to the appetizer table. She looked up to see he had followed her. "Does this other person feel the same way about you?"

"I don't know," he said.

"Well, you should ask her," she said, turning to face him. There was something about the look on his face. He looked so serious.

"Okay, Max. You never do make it easy for me. Here goes. Would you like to go out on a date with me?"

"Me?" Did she just hear what she thought she did?

"Just give me a yes or no and put me out of my misery, please," he begged.

"Yes, of course." She started to giggle for no apparent reason. "Sorry," she said, composing herself. "I just really didn't expect that." She knew she had a huge grin on her face. Detective Cruz had just asked her out on a date!

Before she knew what was happening, he put his arm around her waist and pulled her close to him. She looked around to see who might be watching and Olivia gave her a thumbs up. If Olivia approved, she didn't care what anyone else thought. She looked in Jason's green eyes and then he kissed her. It was just one kiss, but it was enough to tell her that she wouldn't mind kissing him for the rest of her life.

If you enjoyed this book, let others know by writing a review on Amazon or your favorite site. I would be most grateful!

To find out when my next novel is released and find out about specials, giveaways and freebies, sign up for my newsletter at www.karensuewalker.com. Or, you can drop me a line at karen@karensuewalker.com and say hello. I always love to hear from readers like you!

You can also follow me on Twitter @ www.twitter.com/karensuewalker or on Facebook at www.facebook.com/bridalshopmysteries

Thanks for reading!

OTHER BOOKS BY KAREN SUE WALKER

MURDER IN WHITE LACE

MURDER IN CRIMSON VELVET

Made in the USA
Columbia, SC
16 May 2023

16771079R00133